BILLY'S PRAYERS

BILLY'S PRAYERS

Dawn Faye Campbell

Library of Congress Number: 2001117809
ISBN #: Hardcover 1-4010-2162-X
Softcover 1-4010-2161-1

This is a work of fiction. Names, characters, places and incidents either are the product of the author's imagination or are used fictitiously, and any resemblance to any actual persons, living or dead, events, or locales is entirely coincidental.

This book was printed in the United States of America.

To order additional copies of this book, contact:
Xlibris Corporation
1-888-7-XLIBRIS
www.Xlibris.com
Orders@Xlibris.com

CONTENTS

Matt, Andrew, and Lori, my world, thank you for your support. Lori thanks for getting me past the rough. I love you guys.

I need to thank Fred Wessels and Sam Singer for providing editing expertise. Sammy, did you think I'd ever finish? Your daily encouragement kept me going.

And most especially to every child who has ever felt the cold hand of abuse. How I wish I could end the hurt forever. Your collective spirit inspired this story.

I went for a walk yesterday
The sun was blinding against the snow-covered landscape
I thought about You
In doing so I felt the warmth of the sun
But ONLY on my face
The wind, fierce, whipped the lightest flakes of snow,
wildly
Without pattern
It reminded me of You
Making tracks, without leaving a trace
Perfect images but never a face
Knowing, but never seeing a thing
Like the snow that falls in the winter
And rain of the spring
Needed but mostly unwanted
By those of little faith
Not wanting to work hard
But always accepting Your grace
Having it all
Yet, wanting more
Seeking a life of goodness
Without being a bore
Questioning truths
So they might be changed
To fit our perspective
For our own gain
Clouds gather and turn the sky a solid gray
Yellow lights flashing . . . turn to red
My brother steps off the school bus
And above his little head
The sun shines again
I feel the warmth
Deeper than before
Meaning returns
As we exchange smiles
My brother and I
And I thank You silently

CHAPTER 1

It was late October and Indian summer, and the warm autumn breeze was stirring softly, peacefully. They were standing knee deep in the rain-swollen current of Hidden Creek, a refreshing haven for Rita and Billy. The cool muck felt good to Rita's aching, blistered feet as she watched Billy skip rocks across the water. She was amazed at his agility. Swift and precise was each graceful toss. Papa would have been pleased.

"Rita, you won't believe it!" Billy cried. His adolescent voice cracked with excitement. "I just tied Papa's record. Eleven skips!" His face positively beamed.

"You're right, I would have to see that to believe it," Rita baited, fully expecting the indignant look she received. Billy turned away, his lanky frame bent as his childish excitement departed.

"Don't be silly, Knucklehead," Rita cooed, feeling sorry she had teased him so. "You know I'm only kidding."

The boy faced her then, smiling, telling her with his expression that she was forgiven. Returning his smile she watched him as he bent over, his nose just inches above the murky water as he searched for a suitable rock to skip.

After awhile Billy grew tired of skipping rocks and went ashore. He found some sticks at the creek's edge and began a new adventure. Over the sound of his pretending to be a world-famous javelin thrower, Rita heard an indistinct sound coming from behind her, up and over the embankment. Wanting to investigate, yet not willing to endanger Billy, she had to figure out a way to lose him.

1011-CAMP

"Billy," she said, motioning for him to come closer. "How long do you think it'll take you to get home if you run as fast as you can without stopping anywhere? I'll bet you a quarter it will take you longer than fifteen minutes."

"Really?" he breathed, astonished. "A whole quarter?"

"No, a half quarter. They make them now," his big sister joked. "Here, take my watch. It's four-fifteen now. Let's see if you can do it." Knowing Billy's competitive nature, she was sure he'd take her up on the bet. She was right.

"Okay!" he exclaimed as he grabbed for her watch and splashed across the water with it. Rita watched him until he disappeared into the pines. Her heart raced as she listened for the sound again. In her search she became like a predator seeking out its prey.

The creek was more like a gully with tawny grass, thick in spots, along the embankment. Slowly she climbed, straining to hear, hoping she was going in the right direction. As she neared its source the sound became more distinct. It was a moaning, and it became louder, rhythmical almost. Rita stopped, entranced. Nothing could have prepared her for what she saw. She could feel the strength seeping out of her body and knew that if she didn't move quickly, she would probably faint right there. Turning soundlessly, she ran, not caring where she was going. Hot tears spilled forth, blurring her vision, making the wind feel cool against her face. She would never know how long or how far she ran. What stopped her was a vision of Billy standing in the yard, alone. It was with reluctance that she turned back for Billy, knowing she could never leave him.

As she expected, Billy was standing at the end of the drive patiently waiting for her.

"I'll take that quarter you owe me now!" he hollered.

"You'll have to wait awhile to get your quarter, I don't have it on me now," Rita said with a heavy heart when she met up with him. "Can I have my watch back, please?"

"Yeah, when ya give me my quarter," Billy kidded as he handed her the watch. "What took you so long?"

Again, the act that she had witnessed earlier was full-blown in her mind. "I went scouting for deer . . . and lost track of time," she lied, hoping he would drop the subject. "Hey, Billy, let's get upstairs before Daddy Joe . . ." Her words ceased mid-sentence as she felt a prickling sensation along the back of her neck. The look on Billy's face confirmed what she already knew.

"I'm gonna bust your ass, you smart aleck little twit!" Daddy Joe growled, his black eyes fierce with anger.

Before she knew it she was on the ground, her body being twisted in directions she never thought possible. While Daddy Joe's knee dug into her back, his left hand was tangled in her hair, pulling her head back so far it felt as if the muscles in her stomach were going to rip. The blows to her rear were powerful. Yet, what sickened her most was the smell of him, and the sound of his ragged breath.

"Don't you think you're a sneaky one?" he hissed with such vehemence that spit shot out in all directions, some in her face, which made her want to vomit, only there was nothing in her belly to choke up.

"Don't you be going and tellin' about what you saw, Missy. If you know what's good for you, you'll keep that trap of yours shut!" With that he stood up. The girl knew what was coming and closed her eyes, waiting for the blow to connect.

The pain ceased. Darkness overcame her.

****

Worry, an ever-present emotion felt by Helen Welch, seemed to render its mark easily on her delicate features in the way of wrinkles. The worried expression remained on her brow as she rifled through piles of letters, bills and old newspapers. She had looked everywhere for that letter. It was nowhere to be found. She remembered clearly that it had been sent from Arkansas, but where in Arkansas? Options of where it could be danced fleetingly in and out of her thoughts as she wrestled with them and searched her muddled mind for clues. When it came up empty, she decided she must have lost it during one of her all too frequent blackouts. She winced at the thought, and fought the impulse to go downstairs and grab a beer. She wanted so badly to forget everything. She knew she could easily, and the urge to start the proceedings, to have just one beer, threatened to overwhelm her. Regret just about choked her as it knotted tight in her throat. Sometimes she was so wrapped up in the guilt she felt over sins of the past that she found it hard to breathe. She wished she could be a little bit stronger, if not for herself, then for her kids, to protect them. In conjunction she felt herself strengthen at the thought.

"Woman, goddamit!" Joe bellowed. "Get your ass down here and get me a beer!"

The strength that any mother should feel at the thought of threat against her children quickly departed from Helen as she hurried down the stairs and into the kitchen. She hesitated for a moment at the refrigerator.

"Helen!" Joe shouted at the top of his lungs.

Broken, she sighed as she pulled open the fridge, reached inside and grabbed two beers.

****

Rita woke to a faint, musty smell. She felt half frozen as cold shivers radiated throughout her body and she began to tremble. Recovering from a beating such as this was always somewhat difficult, to say the least. Sometimes she could compose herself within minutes, on other rare occasions it took days and constant supervision. It was on those occasions when she would come agonizingly close to reaching Mama, who sadly had locked herself away in the prison of alcoholism.

When she opened her eyes, they were met with darkness. Petrified she searched frantically for some source of light or color, only to come to the conclusion she was blind. Daddy Joe must have knocked the sight right out of her. She could believe it after what he did to her older brother Rick. Rick can't hear out of his left ear and has violent seizures, which she believed were caused by Daddy Joe and Mama too, only because she allowed it to happen.

As she lifted herself to a sitting position, slowly so as not to aggravate her throbbing head, she realized why she wasn't able to see. She was in the cellar. No wonder she was so stiff. She was chilled to the bone. It was pitch dark and she could feel the cold damp earth under her palms as she crawled across the ground to the cellar door. With her fingertips numb she struggled with the latch. She felt anxious, as though she was locked in from the outside, left to rot like the rows of canned tomatoes, with broken seals, forgotten years ago.

Stark fear paralyzed her. Was someone down here with her or was it just her imagination? She could have sworn she heard someone breathing. Finally, she felt the latch give, and with a force she never knew she possessed she opened the door. Sunlight flooded in so bright it brought tears to her eyes, but she was grateful. She would much rather be blinded by sunlight for an instant than blind, period. She looked back into the dark recesses of the cellar and saw Billy, her sweet little protector, fast asleep. His face was red and puffy from crying, his skinny little hands were doubled into fists, and ready to swing if need be. How her heart ached as she watched him sleep. What a fragile little boy he seemed lying there. The things he had to endure on her account. She wasn't sure if she could take it much more. They had everything they needed to make a run for it, except guts. Of course she could always fall back on the "Billy won't leave Mama" excuse. If only she could figure out a way to convince him of the error in his loyalty to her. Mama didn't seem too terribly worried over their troubles, why should they stick around for her, when instead they could find a way to get to Alaska, the last place Papa was seen alive.

"Billy," she whispered, shaking him lightly. He mumbled a little something, tossed and turned, seeming to drift deeper away. He was exhausted, the poor boy. She decided to let him sleep. It allowed her time to think.

As her thoughts drifted, she tried to recall if there had ever been a time since Papa's supposed death when she felt truly safe and secure or even relaxed, but none came to mind. As a child she had all she could ask for and more, but her greatest strength were her parents with their solid morals and their deep religious faith. Her father made a decent living as a well digger, while her mother was content as a homemaker. They had a comfortable country home on three hundred and sixty acres of land. However, what stood out the most was the love. In Rita's opinion the love between her father and mother was unexplainable, and the love and devotion they gave their kids, immeasurable. She guessed that the sweet taste of her pleasing life then, weighed heavily on her judgment of the bitter taste of her life now.

The whole sordid affair began in June 1960, when her father, Richard William Klein, and his best friend, Joseph P. Welch, decided to go to Alaska looking for oil, one of Joe's many get-rich-quick schemes. Rita remembered it vividly, for at the time it sounded to her like a great adventure. She begged her Papa to let her go with him; unfortunately, his answer was no.

Joe had made all the arrangements. They were to travel by train to Seattle; from there they were to take a private plane to Anchorage, to prospect the surrounding area. The entire trip would take at least four months.

Rita remembered Mama being very upset. She did not want Papa to go, said she had a bad feeling about it. But, Mama never liked Papa to go away at all, and if a person had ever seen them together they would understand why. Rita had only been eleven years old at the time, yet, even then, she understood the love displayed by her parents was rare and true. To be separated for any length of time from each other was torture for both of them, but more so for Mama who seemed at her best when they were together.

"Rita, you okay?" Billy's soft questioning voice abruptly brought her back to the present situation.

"Yeah," she answered, beckoning him to sit next to her. He yawned and squinted his sleepy blue eyes against the glare of the mid-morning sun as he plopped down beside her on the cellar steps.

"I definitely feel better than you look," she said dryly. His ebony hair was matted, with an occasional strand or two flaring. He had dark circles under his eyes, making them appear even larger than they were, and his face was still swollen from the previous night's crying. Rita felt a dull pang in the center of her chest as Billy looked up at her with his huge trusting eyes. It made her all the more determined to leave as soon as possible.

"How did I get down here anyhow?" she asked.

Billy hesitated while he yawned, shivered a little and scratched his head. Being half asleep as he was, he stammered. "Well . . . after Daddy Joe went up to the house, madder than hell, Betty came outside. She helped me carry you down here. She said she was tired of you always making so much trouble. Rita, why in the heck does she say that? I get so mad when she does." The youngster complained as hurt and confusion clouded his blue eyes.

"Because she is ignorant!" Rita managed. The anger in her was so powerful it made her shake uncontrollably. "She doesn't use the brains God gave her and she expects me to be just the same. I've got news for her. I will never be anything like her, never as long as I live."

Billy just sat there beside her quietly. His hurt expression remained.

"Oh Billy, I don't know. I guess she tries to be like a mother hen, and she thinks she is helping us when she does stuff like that."

Billy grinned with delight for he was happy with that explanation. He was never one to argue, and didn't like it none when anyone else in the family was so inclined. Then, his face lit up as he jumped up and turned on Rita. "I almost forgot! We're going to Granny and Grandpa Klein's today. Come on, Rita, you have to get ready. Daddy Joe will be pulling a fast one today. Come on. Come on, Rita!" He was clearly excited. Rita, on the other hand, wanted to go hide somewhere. The last thing she wanted to do was to have a race with the devil himself already this morning. However, the idea that she could possibly beat Daddy Joe at his own game made her determined to do just that.

****

CHAPTER 2

Helen woke with a staggering headache. She slipped quietly out of the bed she had begrudgingly shared with Joe the past five years and went to check on the kids. Opening the door to William's room she found it was empty. She headed toward Rita' s room; it too had never been slept in. *Where are they?* She wondered. She hurried downstairs to Betty's room, and opened the door to find her eldest daughter sleeping soundly.

"Betty, wake up," Helen whispered.

"What? What Mama?" Betty mumbled as she sat up in bed. "What's wrong?"

"It's William and Rita, they are gone. Do you know where they are?"

Betty was clearly irritated when she informed her mother, "They said something about spending the night in the pines, at their fort." Betty rolled over, away from what disturbed her slumber.

Helen looked her eldest daughter and saw herself twenty years earlier. "Oh, okay, sorry I woke you dear."

"Can I go back to sleep now?" Betty asked.

"Yes, you do that."

Relief washed over Helen as she shut Betty's door. She took comfort in the knowledge that William and Rita were safely out of the house. She knew they were much safer out in the woods—safer than they could ever be in the confines of Joe's home. She berated herself for giving in and getting drunk last night. She would have to try harder in the future to fight the powerful pull the bottle had over her, if not for herself then for Richard's sake. Thoughts of him surrounded her, making all else seem distant and vague. What if he was still alive? How she wished to know for sure. Deep in her heart, she believed he was. Joe knew more than he would ever say but it was no help to her. What she needed was to find Richard, only before she could accomplish that she would have to find the letter.

"Morning, Mama!" Billy squealed. Helen and Rita both cringed at the sound of his voice as he hurriedly stomped up the stairs to his room.

"Good morning, Mama," Rita mumbled as she walked past her mother. She really didn't know what was so good about it. The two of them looked like death warmed over, each of them having to face their own demons last night, Mama's being alcohol and hers being Daddy Joe. This observation stifled any sarcastic remark that came to mind, and the girl kept on walking up the stairs as her mother called out.

"Rita, the next time you and William decide to spend the night in the pines, I would appreciate it if you would ask my permission beforehand. Is that clear?"

So she thought we spent the night in the pines did she? Shows how much she knows. "I asked you mama . . . you said we could," Rita muttered. She kept her almond shaped eyes downcast for fear her mother would catch her in the lie. Didn't matter how drunk Mama got, she was good at doing that, especially with her. Rita had to bite her tongue to keep from asking why she cared anyway. She had probably been three sheets to the wind last night, for that matter.

"You do know we are going to Grandma and Grandpa's for your birthday dinner today?" Helen reminded Rita. She herself hated going to Richard's parents' home. She knew they were more than a little disappointed with her considering everything she had done since Richard's supposed death—especially since she married Joe. If it weren't for the kids, she would have avoided going there entirely. It was too hard. Too many memories assaulted her there.

Memories of how she used to be—how she used to hold her head up high. So many terrible things had happened since that time, that just holding her head erect was a feat.

Helen looked her daughter over searching for clues as to what might have happened the night before. Sometimes it was hard for her to really look at Rita. The girl took on her father's seriousness, a quality Helen had admired coming from Richard, yet it made her uneasy when she saw it in her daughter, especially when Rita was younger.

"Yes, ma'am," Rita answered, her eyes still downcast. "May I go and clean myself up?" Helen nodded and the girl went.

As she reached the top of the stairs her sisters came upon her. First came Betty whose beauty was only skin deep. She had dark looks and a tiny frame that resembled Mama, but, like Billy, had inherited Papa's striking cobalt blue eyes. Behind her was Sally, a miniature Rita, with thick brown hair and golden brown eyes, her frilly, bubbling personality their only major contrast. Bringing up the rear was Linda, happy as usual, the baby of the family. Her flaming red hair and the cluster of freckles on her cheeks and the bridge of her nose caused everyone who knew her to nickname her "Raggedy Ann." Linda's only failing, though no fault of her own, was the fact that Daddy Joe was her father.

Linda and Sally cheerfully sang "This Old Man" as Betty glared at Rita. "It's about time!" she spat. "I was beginning to think you were going to ruin another perfectly fine day with your irresponsibility. I'm through covering for you, Rita. From now on, you're on your own!"

Betty's words worked like tiny pebbles in a shoe to aggravate Rita. "You, covering for me? What a joke! You wouldn't know the first thing about doing something for someone beside yourself. Or might I be mistaken? Was the act I came upon yesterday an act of chivalry so Mama wouldn't have to suffer through it?" Rita's adrenaline was pumping hard in her veins. "I doubt it! I'll bet you did it to meet your own ends?"

Betty's eyes glazed over. "Oh, you had better watch that mouth of yours, Missy, before I slap it! It ain't none of your business, but I do as I am told, which is more than I can say for you." With that she descended the stairs, her head held high. Rita could only look after her with pity.

In the solitude of her room, Rita wept. She just wanted to curl up into her trusty wool blanket like a silkworm encased in its cocoon. Neutrality, that's what she needed. What she had was about five minutes to get ready or her plan to best Daddy Joe would be ruined. Scuffling to find some decent clothes to wear, she came across Mama's white knit sweater. Mama must have misplaced it when she put the laundry away. Attracting Rita's gaze was the corner of an envelope protruding from the pocket. Being short on time, she slipped the envelope into her stocking, down beneath her heel, then eased on her hand-me-down shoes.

Someone rapped on her door. Before she had a chance to see who entered, Billy barked, "Rita, they're waiting for us in the hall. Hurry!"

Daddy Joe, Mama and Betty looked up at them as she and Billy raced down the stairs. One look at Daddy Joe, and Rita could tell the race was about to begin.

"Well, now isn't this a pleasant surprise," Daddy Joe taunted. "I wasn't expecting to see you this morning. I would have guessed you'd be out like a light, sleeping that is. This causes a slight dilemma. You see I have offered little Ron here a ride to the green bridge over Hidden Creek. You-all know I can't go back on my word, yet your Grandma and Grandpa Klein would be very disappointed if Rita was to miss her own birthday get-together. It brings me to a hard decision. I will allow you ten minutes head start, if you by chance happen to meet up with us at the bridge you'll have yourself a ride; if not, well, I guess we'll see you there in about four hours.

"You have to be kidding me!" Rita shouted. "Mama, help me. You know I'll never make it to the bridge on time," she pleaded with everything she had.

"Thank you for your kindness, sir, but I believe I'll walk. It will do me good," the paperboy stated, seeming a bit confused by the situation.

"Nonsense, boy. You will ride along with us to the bridge. I won't take no for an answer."

"Mama . . . please!" Rita begged.

"Joe, you know as well as I do that she can't make it. Why don't you let her stay here?" Mama asked in a quiet voice.

This surprised Rita. Mama usually kept silent, which is exactly what the girl needed her to be now, or her plans would be ruined.

"Daddy Joe I beg of you to let me stay here. I still have blisters on my feet from the last time. You know I can't make it."

You get your skinny little ass out that door, Missy, before I kick it! Go!" He raised his foot in a kicking motion to make his point.

Out the door Rita flew, slamming the screen door behind her, she heard it open again and glanced back long enough to see Billy with his fingers crossed, giving her a reassuring wink. So far things were going according to plan.

Two weeks earlier Daddy Joe made a similar wager with her. She ended up the loser and had to walk the ten miles to Grandma and Grandpa's. As soon as she got there the kids were rounded up for the ride back. She had been exhausted, hungry and dying of thirst, but she was not allowed to go into the house. Instead, she had to pile in the car with the whole family and go back home. During the week that followed she and Billy spent every free moment they had scouting the area, searching for the fastest route to the green bridge. They knew Daddy Joe, and when he found a new way to torture them he would do the same thing over and over again until it had no effect. They had to be careful, however, because if Daddy Joe thought for one minute that Rita could make it to the bridge on time, he would find a different way to get his kicks.

As she climbed the steep slope leading to the pines, it started to rain. Michigan weather was the funniest thing. A half-hour ago the Sun was shining so bright she could barely adjust her eyes to it. Now gray clouds hovered over head as far as the eye could see, and the wind picked up too, sending an array of fallen leaves whirling around her. As she reached the protection of the pines she was thankful, for the bad weather had slowed her pace. The thickness of the trees and their branches made a fine canopy that saved her from the now howling wind and rain. Instinctively, she cut through the dense section of the pines, the only problem being what she was going to look like afterwards. As it was, Daddy Joe was going to be mad enough to whip her.

She scurried through obstacles on all fours. Low branches grabbed at her clothes and flesh and dead pine needles pricked her unmercifully. Halfway through the densest part of the pines, she came across their hideout, the BT, which is short for the Big Tree. It was a small clearing set deep in the pines where very few humans ventured. It was located on state land they claimed as their own. Quickly, Rita uncovered Billy's safe deposit box, an old rusty milk crate hidden in a pit he had dug. In it were a few potatoes he had swiped from Mama's bin, a baseball and glove, some books and the jewelry box that Papa gave her just before he left for Alaska. Hastily, she opened the jewelry box and plucked out a quarter from the ring section, then placed the box back in the crate, recovered it with dirt and pine needles and resumed her race against the devil.

****

Why did he have to be so damn mean? Helen wondered as she watched Rita dash out the door. She wished with all her heart that she could somehow stop his wickedness. Lately she had gathered enough courage to try, but failed miserably every time. She didn't mind so much when he was cruel to her; she felt she deserved it. However, it killed her each time she watched him play his little games with Rita. It used to be with Rick, her oldest, that Joe played his games with, until Ma and Pa stepped in and sent him off to live with Ma's brother George. *Well,* Helen thought, *if Ma and Pa can do it—so can I.*

"Come on. Lets go!" Joe ordered as everyone piled into the car.

Helen took her sweet time.

"Oh no, Joe, I forgot the birthday cards," she lied. Before he could protest she went back into the house, not once, but twice. On her third attempt, Joe threatened to leave her behind. She decided she might have overdone it a little and settled herself into the front seat of the Buick.

Joe took off and raced toward town, an evil smile stretched across his determined face.

"Joe would you mind stopping at Millie's?" Helen attempted. "I'd like a soda."

The look she received warned her Joe was not in the mood for any more of her tactics. Down the road a bit was the green bridge. He sped toward it. His self-satisfied laugh rang out as he looked toward the bridge—Rita was nowhere in sight.

****

Finally, Rita came to an area where she could stand. She looked down at her watch and felt smug for she was about two minutes ahead of schedule. As she reached the outer limits of the pines, she looked down the steep incline of the hill and saw the green bridge. Then her heart caught in her throat because about a quarter of a mile down the road and gaining fast was the Buick, with Daddy Joe at the wheel. Frantically she looked about. Directly to her right was an old horse-drawn milk wagon she and Billy had converted into a lookout post years ago. She spotted a piece of sheet metal dangling from one of the sides and was hit by a wild idea. She tore that piece of metal off and raced to the edge of the hill. Without further thought she hopped on that piece of metal and rode it down the hill like a sled in winter. How she flew! It was a bumpy ride and she hung on to the curled-up edges like a cowboy would a bucking horse. At the bottom of the hill she crashed into a patch of raspberry bushes. She was alive, however, and ran for that green bridge as though her life depended on it. She saw little

Ron, the paperboy, get out of the car about fifty yards away and called out weakly. The boy heard her but the car started to pull away. She kept running toward it. "Mama . . . Mama," she called out, pitifully. "Wait, wait for me." Suddenly, the car came to a screeching halt making dust fly everywhere, gagging her. The passenger side door opened and Rita jumped in. Her heart was pounding furiously while her lungs burned with each hard gasp for air. Sweat poured from her brow as she situated herself in the back seat between Billy and Linda.

"Mama yelled at Daddy," Linda whispered, bewildered. "She said to him 'Stop the car or I'll jump out!' Now Daddy's mad at her." Linda looked wide-eyed at the couple in the front seat. Rita followed her stare. Daddy Joe had a dark look about him as he slammed the car into first gear and pressed hard on the gas, making the car fishtail down the gravel road. He gave Rita a menacing look in the rearview mirror but was silent, which suited her just fine. She looked toward her mother, and to her amazement she was smiling, something Rita hadn't seen her do in years. Rita arched an eyebrow questioningly at her mother, and Helen winked back. A lone tear fell from her eye, but her smile remained brilliant. At that, Rita's heart leapt with glee, for in her estimation it meant her mother was finally starting to come around.

Next to her, Billy stared openmouthed at her appearance. Rita had to admit she looked a sight. Deep red lines, scratches caused by the thorny raspberry bushes, cascaded down her legs. Mud was caked on her knees and elbows, and her dress was covered with stick-tights and Burdocks. Poor Billy was sincerely worried about her. Appropriately, she remembered the silver in her grasp. Slowly she slid her hand atop Billy's and dropped the quarter she promised him into his palm. With that, her appearance was forgotten and Billy's quarter went directly into his pocket. He could barely contain his smile.

****

CHAPTER 3

The smell of fresh-baked apple pie was in the air as they pulled into the drive at Grandma Klein's house. The car barely came to a stop before the kids started fighting their way to be the first out of the car and the first to sink their teeth into grandma's famously delicious apple pie.

"Hold it!" Daddy Joe roared. The effect of his words had the kids frozen in the oddest positions. "If anyone should ask what happened to Rita, which—mark my words—someone will, it will be said . . ." He hesitated, as his devious little mind went to work thinking up a reasonable explanation. "She went and helped the widow Brown round up some cows that got loose from the pasture." Satisfied with what he had come up with, he looked hard at each one of the kids until he was certain his words had sunk in. As soon as he turned back around they started fighting their way out again. Billy, as usual, was the first to get out and run to the security of Grandma Klein's embrace.

"Happy Birthday, young man; my goodness Billy, how you have grown!" Grandma crooned as she hugged him heartily then scooted him across the porch, through the opened screen door and into the kitchen. Finishing with Billy, Grandma turned to greet the next of the kids, which happened to be Rita.

"Happy Birth . . . my Lord child, what on Earth happened to you?" Grandma asked, concern softening her normally hard-lined face. "Land sakes, Maggie, what happened to Rita?" she scolded, staring hard into Mama's eyes.

011-CAMP

"It's not as bad as it looks, Grandma," Rita said easily, coming to her mother's rescue. "The Widow Brown's arthritis has been acting up again so I offered to help with the chores. As my luck would have it, some cows got loose from the pasture and I had to help chase 'em back."

Absentmindedly, Grandma started rubbing her wrist for fear her own arthritis might take a turn for the worse by the mere mentioning of it. She accepted the girl's explanation reluctantly and then hugged her warmly, yet with a little reserve, for Grandma Klein was a very clean woman who hated dirt and grime and Rita was covered with it. The aroma Grandma carried about her was tantalizing indeed, a mixture of apple pie and homemade bread. It was so heavenly that Rita wished she could stay there wrapped in her grandma's arms forever. However, the thought of the apple pie was making her mouth water so she wiggled herself free and followed the route Billy had taken to the kitchen. She wasn't surprised to find the room empty, the only sign Billy had ever been there was his pie plate with nothing but a few crumbs on it.

Rita sat down and watched the steam roll off the pie as she cut herself a sliver. She took a bite and savored the warm wonderful taste of it as the rest of the family filed in.

"Rita, you should be ashamed of yourself!" Grandma wailed. "Go wash your hands, child."

Rita looked down at her hands and felt so ashamed, because they were filthy. A healthy appetite guided by hunger had a way of taking precedence over manners. Still, Rita felt the heat rise to her face from embarrassment and excused herself from the table and headed straight for the bathroom, only to find Billy locked in it. She tapped lightly on the door.

"Who's there?" Billy called out nervously.

"It's me. I need to wash my hands. You done, or what?"

Slowly, the door swung open enough for her to enter the spacious bathroom. Of all the rooms in the house, this was Rita's favorite. As she shut the door and locked it behind her, Billy whispered excitedly, "Guess what I got?" He bent down and lifted his pant leg to reveal a large knife taped to his leg. "I betcha this was Papa's hunting knife!"

"What else did you get?" Rita inquired as she turned the hot water on full blast, a luxury they didn't have at Joe's house where water still had to be boiled on the wood stove to be made hot. As Billy lifted his pant leg higher, Rita saw two cans of sardines and some baseball cards.

"Well, I got some sardines, some baseball cards . . ." He pulled his pockets out of his pants and, being careful not to drop any, revealed many kinds of hard candy. "I got hard candy and a writing tablet." He patted his belly, making sure the tablet was still in place.

"A writing tablet?"

"Yeah, Granny likes me to write poetry, she says Papa did too, but not as good as me. Oh yeah, I also got some jerky in my other sock."

"Mmm . . . My favorite! I'll see what I got. Maybe we can swap. You better get now. I don't feel like making up an explanation for what we are doing in here together. I'll meet you in the barn later," Rita said as she scrubbed vigorously at the dirt under her nails.

Only when Billy was gone did she go to the linen closet to see her goodies. At the very back of the closet, under the rug, is where Grandma and Grandpa decided they should leave money for her to collect, whenever she could. She did not have a chance to get the money the last time, two weeks ago, so the amount tucked under the rug should be sizable. She found two twenties and a ten dollar bill. Also stashed under the rug were a few sample packets of shampoo and a bar of soap that smelled of strawberries, which would be used as a bargaining tool if she needed something from Betty. She found some masking tape in the medicine cabinet and used it to secure the supplies to her inner thighs. She worked quickly and efficiently. When she looked down at her shoes she was reminded of the envelope in her stocking. She slipped off her shoe and felt her foot to make sure the letter was still there. It was.

She wanted to take it out and open it right there to see what it was all about, but was afraid that she might get caught. Hastily she put her shoe back on and vacated the bathroom. She started down the hall, but stopped mid-way to look at the portraits of her father hanging there, covering a fourth of the entire wall. Papa was Grandma and Grandpa's only child and it stood to reason their lives had revolved around him. They, like Rita, had never accepted their son's death, and their hate for Daddy Joe, the man they held responsible for his missing, consumed them.

Rita gazed lovingly at the portraits. In her opinion Papa was the most handsome man ever to walk the Earth. He was tall and rugged looking. She remembered having to aim for the stars just to look at his face, and a handsome face it was. He always seemed to have a tan that gave his skin a beautiful bronze tone. In her favorite photo of him, his thick auburn hair was slicked back in a fifties fashion. He wore a cool black leather jacket, and a wonderful lopsided grin, the same grin she had seen on Billy's sweet face hundreds of times. Never once had that grin failed to disarm her. At home no one was allowed to display any pictures of Papa. They had to hide the pictures they had of him or Daddy Joe would take them away. Rita remembered the day that she had told Grandma and Grandpa Klein they weren't allowed to have pictures of Papa; actually, it was the day she told them everything.

On that day she had been sick with strep, which was very contagious when you had the fever, so she had to stay home from school. Mama was waiting tables at Millie's, and Daddy Joe needed to conduct some business, as he put it, about selling her Papa's land (in other words, he needed to be rid of her), so he allowed her to stay at her Grandma' s for the day. After he dropped her off, she was spoiled profusely for the whole day. All she had to do was say the word and anything she wanted was hers for the taking. Later in the afternoon while she rested on the davenport waiting for the Mickey Mouse Club to come on, Grandma went to get her a bowl of ice cream. Grandpa sat in his easy chair, half asleep, with an unlit pipe hanging out of his mouth. Rita looked up at the display of portraits of Papa on the wall and began to cry, softly at first, but then uncontrollably as sobs racked her little body.

"Ma, I think you better come here," Grandpa called out, unsure of what exactly was going on.

"What is it, Pa?" Grandma asked as she walked into the living room. Realizing that something was amiss, she dropped Rita's bowl of ice cream on the coffee table and rushed to the girl's side. "What's the matter, child?" she asked as she gripped the child's hands with her own.

"I . . . we aren't allowed . . . we can't have any pictures of Papa," the girl managed to spit out between sobs. "Since Daddy Joe came, we can't have no pictures, no ice cream. I only get ice cream when I come here." This brought on a set of new and violent sobs. Blubbering, the girl continued, "No ice cream, no popcorn, none . . . we . . . none."

Grandma and Grandpa looked at each other, perplexed. "She must be delirious," Grandpa said.

"We can't even watch television when Daddy Joe's home!" Rita wailed. "Ooh, I hate him so. I do! I do! He's mean and evil and I hate him!" she was raging out of control.

"There, there, child. There, there," Grandma said, trying to soothe the girl as she felt her forehead. "She's burning up, Pa. Go get me a cold wash cloth and some ice, will you?" She shooed Grandpa toward the kitchen, then came back to Rita's side. "Now calm down, sweetie, Grandpa's getting some ice. It'll bring your temperature down, but you have to calm down and stay still for me. Okay? Now, what's this you're saying? You mean to tell me you haven't had ice cream in two years? Aren't you exaggerating just a bit? Now, talk so I can understand you. Okay?"

Grandma's voice was soothing and the way she softly touched Rita's forehead with her cool hands seemed to have a calming effect on her. As she helped Rita to a sitting position, the girl started to confess the happenings of the past few years.

"One day . . ." Rita began, "when Daddy Joe first came to live with us, Betty, Billy, Rick and I were watching something on television when he came home. He seemed to be in a foul mood, cause he kept slamming things around. Us kids tried to ignore him 'cause Mama told us to steer clear when he was in a bad mood. Then, for no reason at all, he grabbed me by the hair and started cussin' and saying things like, 'who do you think you are, girl! I saw that grin on your face, you little smartass! You think it's funny that I had a bad day, don't you? Well, I'll show you something really funny.' Then he laughed like he was crazy and he slapped me so hard, I flew across the room and landed on Rick. Rick got mad and jumped to my defense, and for awhile Daddy Joe and him fought like boxers, but Rick started to win the fight so Daddy Joe picked up one of Mama's beer bottles and hit Rick over the head with it. It knocked him out cold. Then Mama came into the room, half drunk already, and it made Daddy Joe madder yet. He told us to get Rick up to his room, any way we could, he was tired of looking at him. We started to do his bidding and he told Mama that we were not allowed to watch that TV anymore. Mama just stood there dumbstruck, so he shouted 'You hear me, woman!' And from that day on we haven't been able to watch television. Except sometimes when he's not home Mama sneaks and lets us watch a program. When the show's over she wipes the set with a cold wash cloth 'cause as soon as he gets home he heads straight for the television and if it even feels warm he'll beat up on Mama or send us kids to bed without supper or something."

One story after another of abuse rattled out of Rita's mouth. The more she told the better she felt, and so she told them everything. "Daddy Joe painted all the windows in Rick's bedroom black," she continued. "Rick is supposed to stay in his room at all times, but he does only if Daddy Joe is home. Daddy Joe tells Mama that Rick has a bad temper that needs to be controlled. That's why he painted his windows black, 'cause it's supposed to have a claming effect or something. Everyday, for some reason or another, he beats up on Rick. Sometimes with a board or tree branch, and then he makes him go to his room—if he isn't there already. One day, when Rick was feeding and watering the dogs,

Daddy Joe unhooked the garden hose and used it to whip him. That was the night Rick started having trouble hearing. He didn't wipe out on a minibike like he told you. He just said that so you wouldn't worry all the time. I'm telling you the truth now because I'm afraid if something doesn't change soon someone's gonna end up dead!"

By the time Rita had finished, Grandpa was so angry and upset that he threatened to get his shotgun to shoot the son-of-a-bitch. Rita knew, of course, that he wouldn't. Grandpa Klein was a kind man who would never hurt another human being, not even one as low as Daddy Joe. Grandma reminded him of his blood pressure and he sat back down in his easy chair, still steaming. But from that night on, Rita noticed that he could not be in the same room with Daddy Joe without fussing and fidgeting or acting distracted. That was the night it was decided Rick would escape by landing a job at the paper mill up north. Daddy Joe disagreed, but Rick was eighteen, an adult, and there wasn't much he could do to stop him. Not more than a week later he was sent to live with Grandma's brother George. Rick tried to get Mama to go too. He begged and pleaded with Mama to move the family up north with him, but she argued that there was no way Daddy Joe would let her take Linda without a fight, a fight that he would surely win. And there was no way she was going to leave Linda behind. She appeased Rick by pointing out that Daddy Joe was mainly mean to him, and things might possibly get better after he left. Of course things got worse, but Rick was never wise to it, her letters to him made sure of that. It was also decided that night, that Betty could not be trusted anymore because Daddy Joe and her got along too well. So, only Billy and Rita would get supplies when they could, and as soon as they had what they needed they would leave home. That was their plan anyway. It had been almost two years since that night, and in Rita's opinion, the time to leave was at hand.

Rita finished admiring the portraits of her father on the wall and decided to go meet Billy out in the barn like she said she would. Instead of going through the kitchen, she snuck out the back, avoiding another run-in with Daddy Joe. As she followed the well-worn path to the barn, lost in her thoughts, something disturbed her. She looked about, trying to figure out what made her feel uncomfortable. She noticed that the chicken coop door was ajar, which was no big deal it just seemed odd. Slowly, she walked toward the coop as a feeling of doom, so powerful she could barely breathe, swept over her. She ran and jumped over the chicken wire fence and through the open coop door to find Betty hanging there, her limbs jerking convulsively as she dangled from a rope knotted around a sagging plank. The rope she used was tied tightly around an old two-by-four that seemed ready to bust from the weight of her, which, in turn, made Rita think it would not hold her weight also. Rita jumped up and grasped the rope above Betty's lifeless head and, just as she had thought, the plank broke with the force of her added weight. She landed on top of Betty as they hit the ground.

"Dear God, please help me!" Rita begged as she loosened the noose that was preventing precious oxygen from reaching Betty's lungs. Her own heart was beating frantically as searched for her older sister's pulse. She felt a faint one at Betty's neck, which was already swollen and discolored beyond the point of recognition.

"Oh, Betty, why?" Rita cried. "How could you do this to yourself?" She was afraid to leave for fear Betty would die before she found help, but she had to do something. When she laid Betty back on the ground her older sister's eyes fluttered, then opened. "Betty, can you hear me?" Rita asked. She crouched down so she would be able to hear a reply.

"Rita . . . is that you?"

"Yes," she said as she smoothed Betty's hair back. "Yes, Betty, it's me. I'm going to go get help now. Don't try to move. Okay? I'll be right back."

"No, please don't go. Don't leave me, Rita."

"Betty, I'm afraid if we don't get help fast something awful will happen." Her sister's color scared her. "Oh God, Betty, why did you do it?" Rita wailed, overcome with emotion. "Why didn't you just leave home? You could have went to Uncle George's . . ."

"And leave the girls? Joe said as long as he had me he'd leave the rest of you alone." Tears of frustration trickled down the elder girl's cheeks. "And not only that, do you know how many times I watched Rick, who is much stronger than me, cower in fear when Joe taunted him? I could not stand up to that. If I left home, what would I do? I have no skills. I mean, I quit school to stay home and play mama. I am too weak. I have watched you and Billy go hungry enough to know I couldn't handle it. And that's exactly what I would be if I left home, hungry and homeless!" She coughed weakly. "Oh Rita, you wouldn't understand, you're different. I hate myself for what I do. I'm mixed up—I thought I was doing the right thing. I'm so awful, I feel so dirty. I hope God forgives me. I can't believe what I've let him do to me." Betty found it difficult to swallow. "Oh gawd, I feel sick . . .can you ever forgive me, Rita?" She cried. "I wouldn't blame you if you couldn't."

"Betty, come on, forgive you for *what*? You were scared, you didn't know any better." Rita choked back tears. "I have no room to talk Betty, I'm still here. I could have left a long time ago, but I was scared, just like you. None of this is your fault."

"But it is . . ." Betty whispered as she reached out to her little sister.

As she did so, Rita saw blood trickle down the side of her mouth. The mere sight of it sent her panicking. "Oh, I have to get some help!" she cried. She left Betty there with her arms outstretched. The scene left a picture in her mind that would be etched in her memory forever. Numbly, she ran out of the coop. Her brain seemed not to be functioning properly as she stood out in the middle of the backyard, screaming, hoping anyone within hearing distance would come to help her dying sister Betty. The blood she saw trickle down the side of Betty's mouth was a sure sign of some kind of internal injury. Her beautiful sister Betty, the same sister who only a day ago she thought she hated, now, powerfully, she realized how very much she loved her. She had probably bled to death slowly while trying to explain her actions. This crushed Rita. "Help! Mama, Grandpa, Help me!" She screamed, as the world around her started spinning. Billy was the first to come, with Grandpa not far behind him. "Billy, get up to the house and call an ambulance. Betty tried to, or, uhm, Betty's hurt bad. Hurry!" Like a flash Billy was gone, no questions asked. Grandpa, on the other hand, was an entirely different story.

"What happened? Where is she? Take me to her," Grandpa snapped, his comprehension of the dire situation showed on his face. " This is not the time to be losing your speech, child! Where is Betty?"

Rita pointed in the direction of the chicken coop. Grandpa understood and went directly. She had done all she could and her body knew it, for as soon as it seemed Betty was in good hands, Rita collapsed. Everything went black.

****

"Mama! Granny!" Billy screamed as he ran into the house. "Call an ambulance . . . Somethin' real bad is wrong with Betty."

Helen's face turned ashen, "What? Where?"

Grandma called the operator while a frantic Helen followed Billy out to the coop, and rushed inside to Betty.

"Pa is she okay?" Helen cried.

"I don't know Maggie."

Billy poked his head inside the coop and nervously announced, "There is something wrong with Rita too."

"You go to her Maggie, I'll stay with Betty." Pa prodded, as he looked into her eyes. "Maggie, go to your daughter, she needs you."

Rita lay unmoving as Helen looked her over. She found several articles taped to the inside of her daughter's thighs. *What in the world?* She wondered as she quickly removed the items before Joe saw them. "Here, William, get rid of these things," she directed as she handed them to Billy. She could not believe what was happening. Through the hazy effects of her hangover everything seemed muted as her perception faded with the sensory overload. Suddenly, one thing became very clear: The unexpected turn of events provided the perfect opening to leave Joe.

****

CHAPTER 4

Somewhere in the distance Rita heard sirens. Was she in an ambulance? She felt the vibration of a vehicle moving under her. And sirens; she kept hearing sirens. Was she dreaming? No. She *was* in an ambulance. She did not need an ambulance, Betty did. What was going on? She tried to sit up but was stopped by a firm hand.

"Hold it right there, Missy," Daddy Joe said sweetly. "It seems you've had a little accident of some sort and need to be examined. Did you get that bruise on the left side of your head when you fell down the cellar steps the other day?" he asked, as nicely as his wickedness allowed. When she didn't immediately answer yes, he grasped her hand roughly with his. "Is that what happened?" He squeezed her hand hard.

"Yes!" she spat, biting back tears. "Yes, that happened the day I fell down the cellar steps. Where is Betty?"

"I'm here," Rita heard Betty whisper. Her head jerked at the sound of it. Then a strange voice interrupted.

"Okay ladies, you better save your energy for the many tests you'll be receiving when we arrive at the hospital."

Rita's mind was assailed by questions. Was Betty going to be okay? Where was Mama? What tests was the strange man talking about? She did not need any tests done on her. The voice must have been referring to Betty when it spoke of tests. She also wondered who that deep velvet-sounding voice belonged to. She tried to see just exactly who was speaking, but was unable to turn her head quite that far. Daddy Joe sat next to her acting like the doting stepfather, his close proximity fraying her already shot nerves. What she would give to get him away from her. Then it came to her.

"Ohhh, it hurts! Help . . ." she groaned, trying to sound as agonized as possible, tossing and turning her head with every wail that she let out. "Please!"

With that, Daddy Joe was asked to sit next to Betty, while the stranger came to check on her.

"Where does it hurt young lady?" The stranger asked.

This man had the most beautiful green eyes Rita had ever seen. It seemed to her that he was looking into her soul. "My, uh, my ear." she stuttered.

He grasped her head with his very large, rough-looking hands and he held her head in check firmly, yet tenderly.

"Which ear?"

"The left one."

"Hold still, while I have a look," he said as he reached across her to a panel that held a bunch of instruments. He held in his grasp an odd looking one, and she jumped when he stuck it in her ear. "Well now, if I thought you'd be afraid of a little otoscope I would have warned you of its coming." He laughed. It was a beautiful sound, his laugh. "Now hold still, please."

As he attempted to find what was causing her so much discomfort, Rita could tell that he was not used to doing this kind of examination. "Are you a doctor?" she asked.

"No."

"You're not a doctor?" She raised her brow. "Do you have any medical experience that would qualify you to be examining me like you are?"

"When you fell down the cellar steps, you hit your head, right?

"I can't remember." *Gracious his eyes are beautiful,* she thought.

"But you clearly remember falling down into the cellar?" he asked, seeming very serious, but there was a playful expression in his eyes

"Yes. Are you going to answer my question?"

"No."

"No, you are not going to answer my question, or no, you do not have any medical experience?"

"I am qualified to do CPR. Does that answer your question?"

"No," she pouted.

Before she could say another word the ambulance stopped. In the minutes that followed, hospital personnel swarmed the ambulance and took her away from the man with the beautiful green eyes. Incredibly, Betty was walking when Rita finally caught sight of her. This knowledge only added to her confusion. Daddy Joe remained at Rita's side while she was wheeled down the hospital corridor.

"Excuse me, sir, you will have to go to the nurse's desk to answer a few questions," ordered a young woman in a starched white uniform. "It's down the hall and to your left. When you're through you're welcome to come sit in the waiting room until we finish examining your daughter."

"Stepdaughter," Rita corrected, bracing herself against the look of pure hatred she received from Daddy Joe. He smiled sweetly at the nurse in acknowledgment, then did as she directed.

"Why am I being X-rayed?" Rita asked the young woman, hoping to find out what exactly was going on. "My sister Betty should be getting X-rays, not me."

"Your sister is in the process of being X-rayed at this very moment; you are correct about that. As for you not needing an X-ray, I'd like to know what makes you so sure. According to your chart, you fell down into the cellar the other day, causing this," she said, pointing to the bruised spot on the side of Rita's head. "We need to snap some rays in order to see how the fall may have hurt you on the inside." She pointed to a door on the other side of the room. "Inside the bathroom there's a closet filled with gowns. I need you to strip down to nothing but your socks, slip a gown on, then sit yourself back down in this chair and we'll get started," she said as she helped Rita up from the chair. "By the way, my name is Judy. I see your name is Rita. May I call you that?"

"Yes," Rita stammered.

"Good. Now go on into the bathroom and undress."

When she closed the door behind her, Rita could feel the heat rise to her face as she felt for the supplies that had been taped to her inner thighs. As she had suspected, they were gone, except for the money; Daddy Joe probably found them, or witnessed them being found. There was nothing she could do about it now except suffer the consequences, so she began to undress. Then she remembered the letter she had stuffed into her stocking. Quickly, she tore off her shoe and felt her foot and to her relief it was still there. She unfolded it and read:

> Mrs. Klein,
>
> I have reached my destination safely. Upon my arrival I learned of a few discrepancies on the subject of your interest. I have to say that I am somewhat puzzled. I will fill you in at your convenience on the details of my findings.
>
> Bucky Rivers

The contents of the letter only confused her. The name Bucky Rivers, however, rang a bell. Where had she heard that name before? Having no answers, she returned the letter to the envelope, noticing, for the first time, the stamped cancellation on the front of the envelope. The letter was mailed from Jonesboro, Arkansas? Now she needed only to find out who Bucky Rivers was, and why he had sent the note.

Hastily, she tied the flimsy gown in the back while looking down at her stocking to make sure the letter and the money could not be noticed. Only when she was positive they could not, did she leave the sanctuary of the bathroom. As she returned to the other room Judy patted the back of the wheelchair as a hint for her to sit there.

"Okay, Rita, have you ever had an X-ray taken?"

"No."

"Okay, honey, first, you have to be very still while it's being done," Judy said as she draped something gray over Rita. "We'll put this smock on you to protect the rest of your body from radiation."

In one second flat Rita was up and bound for the door. Judy must have learned her like a catchy phrase for she was right behind her. She caught her at the door and prevented her from opening it.

"Radiation? Thanks, but I don't need an X-ray."

"Listen, Rita, I know you're scared, but honey, having an X-ray taken will not hurt you. Besides, if you won't cooperate we'll have to restrain you," she said, her voice comforting yet stern. "Now come and sit."

Reluctantly Rita did what the nurse asked, but not before letting her know exactly how appalled she was at her accusation of her supposed fear.

"I am not afraid," Rita declared bravely. "If you knew me you'd be laughing at yourself right now. But, radiation was scary. Having read enough about it to have a healthy respect for it, she feared it, but the nurse didn't need to know it. "I mean, I've been through more than you'll ever know, and I've always been ready to face whatever comes my way."

After she had her say the rest of the examination went smoothly. She had to admit she could learn to like Judy. The fact that the nurse seemed to have her pegged without acting high and mighty about it was reason enough for her to halfway like her.

At last Judy took the heavy smock off her and told her she could get dressed. "I'll wheel you down to another room where the doctor will examine you," she said. "It will probably take awhile because the doctor is running behind."

"You mean to tell me they have only one doctor at this hospital," Rita complained, unable to believe it possible.

Judy laughed at the girl's ignorance and went on to explain there was only one physician on hand in the emergency room while there were many other physicians on call, ready to be here at a moment's notice.

The room Rita was taken to seemed small compared to the

X-ray room, and it was well lit. It took her a moment to adjust her eyes to the brightness of it. It seemed bare and cold, and the smell alone made her light-headed.

"Like I said, Rita, it will be awhile before the doctor checks in. Let's get you on the table." She pointed at what looked like a bed to Rita. "Let me help you." After helping Rita up on the table, the nurse told her, "I'll be back in awhile to see how you're doing." With that, she left.

Rita hadn't realized how exhausted she was and within minutes was fast asleep.

It seemed like she had just fallen asleep when she was awakened by Judy's soft voice. "Wake up, sleepy head."

"I'm awake," Rita said, like a bear.

"I hate to wake you with bad news, but Dr. Jennings says you're going to have to put the gown back on so he can examine you thoroughly." Judy held the gown in her arm, then handed it to Rita.

"Examine me for what?" Rita complained. She was a bit irritated that she had no control of what was happening. "So I have a bump on my head from falling down some stairs. I'm fine now. Don't you think that I would know if there was something seriously wrong with me?"

"It's more than a bump, Rita."

"Okay! Give or take a few bruises. What do you expect? I fell into the cellar."

"Breaks and fractures that have healed months, maybe years ago! I would say they are a little more serious than a few bumps and bruises."

"What? Well I, uh, I've got a bad attitude that tends to get me in a lot of trouble. I used to get in fights all the time at school. You ask . . . Look, I don't have time for this!"

"Listen, Rita," Judy said, cutting her off. "It's time for you to hush up and do as you're told. Why, anyone with half a brain can tell just by looking at you that something very wrong is going on and it needs to be stopped. I personally am not usually the meddling sort, yet I will not now or ever stand for the abuse of a child." Judy cupped Rita's face in her hands as tears welled in her eyes. "It is important that you understand, Rita, nothing can be done without proof. That is what this examination will provide."

Rita picked her words carefully. "Let's say I allow you to examine me, what exactly will it prove? I'll be eighteen tomorrow, isn't it a little too late for this? It's not like I'm a little child unable to protect myself. Why don't you reach out and help the kids who really need it. I appreciate your concern and all, only I feel it would be better spent saving others. The little ones, or the ones where it ain't so damn obvious. Like the kids taking the blows where there are no physical signs. You know, when the words and acts of a person work like a never ending hailstorm, and the shit keeps pelting but there are no bruises, only a constant sting. Help those kids! With me you see the signs, but five years too late. And if your logic is to fix the abuser by placing blame starting with me, well, can this exam prove who is doing the abusing? I mean, you said yourself you could tell just by looking at me that there was something terribly wrong. Can this examination prove who's doing the wrong? If so, I'm all for it; otherwise, I think I'll be going home now."

"Sorry, Rita, you won't be going home. We have permission from your stepfather to examine you thoroughly. He has already informed us to expect your unwillingness to be examined." Judy grasped Rita's hands as she continued to speak with urgency. "Please, stop protecting her! I know you think you're doing good by her, but in reality, honey, you're just making things worse. The problems your mom has, the drinking and all, they're not going to go away, and unless she gets help the abuse will continue."

Rita was not surprised by Judy's words; in fact, she halfway expected them. She was, however, upset that the nurse fell into that deceitful web of Daddy Joe's just when she was beginning to like her.

"Oh, you're right. I can't take it anymore! I'll do anything, anything it takes. Just help me! Help us all!"

She began to cry. She was acting of course, even though the

flow of tears came easily. In the end, it was no longer an act but an outlet for the pain and frustration she felt, knowing Daddy Joe would always have the upper hand. Judy held her as she cried and when her tears were spent she helped her to stand and offered her a gown "Everything is going to be okay. Don't you worry."

"Judy," Rita began, as she walked to the counter and grabbed a few tissues. "Do you know anything about Betty?"

"Yes, as a matter of fact, I just looked in on her. She's down the hall, sleeping like a baby."

"But she was bleeding. Blood was coming out of her mouth, and doesn't that mean there are internal injuries? I mean, I thought . . ." Rita was astonished.

"She bit her tongue," Judy said. "That is where the blood came from. She's going to be just fine, physically. Mentally, that's another story."

"But her neck. It was all swollen," Rita thought, aloud.

"The swelling will go down. She may or may not be scarred from the rope burns. All in all, she fared pretty well considering what could have happened." Judy turned for the door. "I'll let the doctor know you're about ready." Then she left as abruptly as she had come.

Two seconds later Rita was out the door behind her. *Run!* Her mind screamed. *Get away, as far away from this place as possible. Don't let Daddy Joe pin this one on Mama,* she thought. *Get out of here while the examining table is still warm.* Yet, she could not just leave; not without seeing Betty. Before she could go she would have to find her sister, and see for herself that she was okay.

Quietly Rita slipped through the dimly lit hall searching, poking her head into every room that looked occupied. It only took a few moments to locate Betty a few doors down from the room she had just put to use. She went directly to the bedside and shook her sister softly awake. "Betty . . ." she whispered.

"Huh . . . what," Betty murmured. "Where am I? Oh." She felt dizzy when she tried to sit up. "I thought it was a dream . . . I was hoping it was all just a bad dream." She turned pale as the event that brought her to the hospital was remembered. "Rita, what did I do?"

"Shhh." Rita patted her head soothingly.

Betty closed her eyes in shame, then whispered, "What are you doing here?"

"I'm running away." Rita decided for sure, right then and there. "Daddy Joe is trying his best to pin this on Mama and I'm not going to let him. He's got them thinking she's the one beating the hell out of us. Can you believe it? And Mama's not here to defend herself. I don't know where she is. So I'm leaving. I know Mama is not completely innocent, but I'm not going to let her take the fall for Daddy Joe. I'm going to find a pay phone so I can call and warn her of what he's doing.

"But I had to see you first to make sure that you were okay." Rita paused for a moment to gain composer. "Do you remember when we were little, back when I was in Mrs. Cook's first grade class, and we were learning about mouth-to-mouth resuscitation? I was so proud that I knew something you didn't—and I asked you if you wanted to learn how to do it. Do you remember? You said sure, so I told you to hold your breath until you die. You thought I had lost my marbles, but you trusted me, so you tried. Of course you couldn't do it; it's just not natural. So I decided to help you along a little by holdin' my hand over your mouth. You remember? You struggled, but I was bound and determined to show you what I'd learned that day, so I kept my hand where it was. Eventually you fainted, although neither one of us knew it at the time. We both thought you had died . . .that I had killed you. Needless to say, I forgot all about mouth-to-mouth!" Rita laughed a little through her tears. "All I could do was blow big puffs of air into your face. You were only out for a few seconds, but it seemed like forever to me. When you woke up you were crying, and you said you were going to tell Papa that I killed you. I begged you not to. I figured if you told on me, Papa would cut a switch. You never did tell on me, and you've been good to me for the most part." Rita's voice was filled with emotion as she continued. "The point is, everyone makes mistakes. Let me clarify that some mistakes are worse than others, and some mistakes can't be undone like going and killin' yourself or *someone else for that matter.*" They both smiled at her meaning. "Thank heaven, sometimes it doesn't go off as planned, and we get a second chance. You've got yourself a second chance here. Take it. The girls need you and so do Billy and I. You've been more of a mother to us kids than Mama has all these years since Daddy Joe's been around. I just wanted you to know that. You do know that, don't you?" They were crying, "We need you, Sis."

"Get out of here you little brat," Betty cried sweetly. "Hurry, before someone catches you. Go! Warn Mama!"

"I love you, Betty."

"Love you too," Betty softly replied. "Now, go!"

Rita kissed her older sister on the forehead then turned for the door and opened it slowly. She peeked outside and down the hall and looked both ways to make sure it was all clear for takeoff. Then she glanced back at Betty. When their eyes met, Rita noticed a different kind of look in her elder sister's eyes. Determination, maybe. Whatever it was, it made her conclude that everything concerning Betty was going to be okay.

She closed the door softly behind her. At the end of the hall she saw a sign that read "stairs" and figured it would be a discreet exit. Once outside, the fear of being caught left her and she began to concentrate on how to get hold of Mama. She wasn't sure how, for all she knew the authorities might have put her in jail, and taken the kids away behind her.

When she looked up across the street, she knew the good Lord was on her side, for Billy was standing there waving his arms like a baby bird, flapping its wings, attempting to fly for the first time.

"Thank you, Lord!" She prayed as she ran to meet Billy.

"Come on, Rita! Aunt Alberta's at the filling station waiting for us!" he called out over his shoulder.

She followed him without asking any questions. Billy knew

what he was doing, and just watching his confident stride satisfied her.

****

"Ma, why did Rita have those things taped to her thigh?" Helen asked pointedly.

Grandma Klein gave her a hard look before returning, "If you hadn't been so drunk on your ass all the damn time, you'd know why. You should've found your courage long before now. I don't know who you think you are, coming into my house and talking to me this way, but I won't stand for it, Maggie, and you know it."

Helen did know it too; many times it kept her from saying what she really felt. Not any longer, she decided. Today things were different. Already she had stood up to Joe and won. That fact alone strengthened her. Still, she was very intimidated by Richard's mother, but realized she must confront her. "Ma, I know that my actions today have been long overdue. I'm sorry about that. But I'm doing something now, okay? I have a plan, but I'm going to need your help! Please start by telling me everything you know."

"Pa and I have been giving Rita money so they could get out of that hell hole of Joe's. I don't know what that crazy son of a bitch has over everyone in this town, and I don't really care. What I do care about are those kids. I don't know all that ever went on at Joe's place. I can say that I do know more than I care to . . .and all of it's bad. How in the hell you ever let that man do what he's gone and done to those kids is beyond me. But judging you for it now won't do any good, so I won't. I was, and still am, very disappointed in you. Since the day Richard brought you home, I took you in as my own flesh and blood, you were the daughter that Pa and I never had. We both had a lot of hopes for you Maggie . . . you let us down."

Grandma Klein looked away for a moment. She looked again at Richard's wife and wanted to cry. What had happened to the little bit of a girl Richard brought home with him so many years ago? Now, standing across from her was a woman she did not recognize. Overindulgence comes with a price, and Maggie paid dearly. Like unpolished silver, the beauty that once radiated from her core had dulled. It seemed so sad. Grandma Klein was grateful to see some spirit in the girl this day, and wanted very much to believe in her. She eyed her skeptically before inquiring, "So, what's this plan of yours?"

"A while back I overheard Joe talking to Daphne, they were talking about Richard."

Grandma Klein visibly tensed at the mention of Daphne's name. That woman was nothing but trouble. The feelings that thoughts of her aroused were intense enough to start a riot. "What the hell does she have to do with this?"

"Ma, I think she is holding Richard somewhere against his will." Helen breathed. It was so strange saying it out loud.

"My boy . . ."

"Yes Ma . . . I know he's alive." Relief washed over Helen as she recognized faith in Richard's mother's eyes. "Daphne lives somewhere in Arkansas, and if you would just help me out a little, I know I could find her. I have a friend who has promised to do whatever I ask concerning this, but before I can do anything I'm going to need to get away from Joe. And, we'll have to find a way to get him to allow Linda and Sally to stay here. I've sent William with Alberta to go get Rita at the hospital, if they can. That friend I was telling you about has a trailer set up in the pines by Hidden Creek. Rita and William are going to stay there. The more spread out we are, the more confused Joe will be. Maybe when he gets back from the hospital you could tell him I took off—just up and left. Act like you're madder than hell at me, I don't care. Tell him you'll look after the girls for him until he finds me and gets this whole mess taken care of."

"I wondered why you didn't go to the hospital with the girls." Mrs. Klein looked appreciatively at Helen before she added, "You've been thinking on this for some time, haven't you?"

"I haven't had the chance to do a thing! Joe's been watching me like a hawk. It doesn't help that I have been a drunken fool, but I'm working on that too. I figured Joe would be good and worried about the girls being checked out at the hospital. I have no doubt he will blame it on me. But that's fine. As long as he's occupied for awhile, I don't care what he does. What do you say Ma? Are you with me?"

Grandma Klein shook her head in amazement and said, "Landsakes Maggie, it's good to have you back." She grasped Helen's hands as she added, "I'll do whatever it takes."

****

When Alberta saw the kids coming around the corner she started her engine. Then she leaned over and opened the passenger side door and hollered, "Come on child. We must get from here!"

Billy and Rita jumped into the moving pick-up and away they went.

They rode in silence through the city. It seemed Alberta and Rita were afraid to speak and Billy was simply too tired. After awhile Billy rested his head in Rita's lap and dozed off.

"I'm goin' to take you home, child," Alberta started. The expression on her cocoa colored face left the whites of her eyes to stand out starkly in the darkness. "We gotta get your money. I can tell you your ma's dead set on believing that your pa's livin'. She is. She's gone to find 'em. Your sisters, all 'cept Betty, are staying with your pa's kin. Your ma wants ya to care for your brother, same as always. Don't worry 'bout Betty, they'll be watchin' 'er close. Joe'll be leaving 'er alone. He'll be aiming', probably to come after you. That's why we're all gonna hide ya 'til your ma comes for ya." she finished, her mouth rattling so fast Rita had trouble comprehending it all.

"Mama knew about the money? How come she never told me she believed Papa was alive? Where is she going to look for him? I want to go with her." Questions poured out of Rita's mouth. "Aunt Alberta, how did you become involved in all this?" she asked.

"Your ma, she just up and told me one day while she wuz visitin'. Told me how she believed your pa might still be living, and that she be thinkin' Joe, he might know more than he's saying. I told her if she ever needed me to help her do anythin', all she haft to do is ask me. She up and called me today . . . asked me if I would help. I 'spect I owe my life to your ma for she got me off the streets. I love her like a sistuh. I do hope your pa is livin' like she thinks he is. It wud bust her heart if he ain't."

"I hope he is too!" Rita agreed, vigorously." Did you like Papa?"

"Yes, I shore did. Even though he be the craziest man I ever did know . . . and I do mean that in a good way. Why, I 'member the first time I ever laid eyes on 'em. He was the cream of the crop. He shore was a looker. And he was so reckless, just a wild thang. 'Course your ma, she be more mannered, and when they first met she shore didn't give him the time!"

"She didn't! I don't believe that," Rita declared. "Tell me more, Aunt Alberta."

"Well, did your ma—did she ever tell you 'bout how your pa . . . how he finally got her to go courting wid 'em?"

"No. Mama never talks to me about stuff like that," Rita pouted. "I wish she did. I could sit and listen to stories about Mama and Papa all day if someone had a mind to tell me."

"Well, you know your ma lived at that old folks home in town, didn'ctha? After her folks went and died."

"Yes."

"Well, your crazy fool of a pa rode his motorized—cycle up in that house, and up them stairs, smack-flat-dab into your ma's room. Mind you child, this is an old folks home. Then he tells your ma he's not leaving 'til she gets on his motorized—cycle wid 'em, so's that he can take her out."

"What did Mama do?" Rita breathed, astonished that Papa had done such a thing.

"She went wid 'em. She says that she did it 'cause she felt like she owed it to them old folks to get your pa outta there. But I be thinking she shore fancied him from the start. She was just too shy. Yep, your ma loved your pa from the start, and still does. That's why she's off to find him."

"Mama must have good reason to believe that Papa is alive if she's willing to go look for him. Did Daddy Joe give her something to go on?"

"All I know is what I told ya, child." shot Alberta. "Ya ask too many questions!"

Rita could tell she was making Alberta nervous so she decided to let her calm down before she asked anymore questions.

When they pulled into town, Alberta decided it would be best to call out to the house to see if Joe was there. Millie's Restaurant was open so they stopped there.

"Me and your brother . . . we'll stay out here. Don't you be lolly-gagging around." Alberta handed her a dime and the girl went on her way.

When she turned the corner of the restaurant she heard the murmur of voices coming through the window. She stopped and put her ear up to it to have a listen.

"She isn't exactly innocent, if you ask me! Always purring around with that sweet little mouth of hers."

There was no mistaking who was doing the talking. Sheriff Vanderpool was making his opinion known to all who would listen. It seemed like someone was asking him questions, the voice being so quiet Rita couldn't make out the words. Then the sheriff piped in again, "They've been having relations for about a year. I knew that sooner or later she'd be with a baby in her belly—any fool would." He laughed hoarsely and continued, "The man who thought he had it all . . . the beautiful wife, the sweet and pretty stepdaughter, Joe should've known it wasn't going to last. He'll be paying for it now, since the girl tried to hang herself on account she's pregnant with his kid."

"Liar!" Rita screamed, as she ran into Millie's. The sheriff didn't have time to stand before she was on him, her fists a-flying. "You take that back, you no-good lying bastard!" She kept hitting him and through her frenzy, in what seemed like slow motion, she saw him reach for his gun. Before she knew it the sheriff was laying face first on the floor as a result of the blow he had received from the man he had been talking to.

"She's a woman, for pete's sake! Unarmed at that!" The man roared, then he turned on her. "You could have been killed! Of all the dumb stunts I've seen in my life, this one takes the cake."

Even before she saw his face she knew who he was. It was the handsome young man with the beautiful green eyes who assisted her in the ambulance. Rita would never forget the deep sound of his voice. And the fact he believed her to be a woman sent a wondrous feeling through her. He had a fierce look about him until his eyes met hers, then his expression changed. "Little girl, you have to think before you act."

Little girl. That hurt. Rita ran out of Millie's. She heard the man follow behind her and it didn't take long for him to catch up to her. "Where do you think you're going?" he snapped.

"Please let me go!" she cried. She noticed that he was wearing a uniform with a badge that read 'State Police'. "You're a police officer?"

"No . . . I am dressed up for Halloween." He bit off sarcastically. "Yes, I am an officer. Aren't you supposed to be at the hospital? What are you doing back in town?" He waited for her to answer.

"I came to get some things from home. My brother Billy and I are going away for awhile."

"Where are you going, and how are you going to get there?" He let go of her as he again waited for her to answer.

"It's really none of your concern." Rita continued to walk away.

"Look, if you're not going to cooperate, I'm going to have to book you."

"For what?" she laughingly demanded. Although allowing this man to book her might prove to be worthwhile.

"I don't know, but give me a minute, and I'll think of something . . . Look, I'm concerned about your well being, that's all."

"I'll be fine. I'm not alone. I'm with an old friend of the family,

Alberta Fox. She and Billy are waiting for me behind the post office. I better get back there or they'll be worried," she assured.

"If you don't mind, I'll see you to her."

Reluctantly Rita agreed, hoping all the while that Alberta would stay calm and not do anything rash when she saw them.

As soon as they turned around Alberta was standing there with a sleepy Billy at her heels. "We ain't got time to waste," Alberta exclaimed. "Joe done parked at the bar. We gotta get your money and go before he gets home!" she finished, obviously unmoved by the presence of the police officer at Rita's side. "Don't ya be standin' there!" she cried.

"I'll keep him here for as long as I can," the police officer snapped. "You keep a cool head, Alberta. Get Rita and Billy safely tucked away. When you're finished, drive down past the bar and honk once if everything's okay; twice, if you need me to keep him occupied longer."

"What in the world?" Rita was stunned. "You guys know each other?" She stood there with her hands on her hips.

"Here you go actin' like a mule. I wish that for once in your life you would do as your told. Now get your fanny in that truck 'fore ya make me mad!" Alberta scolded as she tugged on the girl's arm.

Rita stood there stomping her foot. "I'm not going anywhere!" Before she had time to blink the officer had her over his shoulder and was walking toward the truck.

"Just listen to Alberta for now. We will explain everything to you in time," he counseled, then dropped her down beside the truck and continued. "I have to get over to the bar before he leaves." Without looking at her he spun on his heels and left. For awhile she stood there looking after him, feeling like an imbecile.

"Get in here, child! Let's get!" She heard Alberta shout over the sound of the truck's engine.

Rita slammed the door as she got into the truck and gave Alberta a glare that would have knocked her down had it been a punch in the nose.

"Don't you go poutin 'bout it now, Rita. It won't do you any good. We'll 'splain everything soon enough."

"This whole thing makes me so mad. If I had been aware of Mama's feelings on the subject of Papa, all this time we could have been working together! If Mama felt Papa was still alive, why did she go and marry Daddy Joe? I know why. All she cares about is herself . . ."

"Don't you go bad-mouthin' your ma, child. She had her reasons for doing what she went and done. You don't know all that you be thinking you know. If you did, you shore wouldn't get yourself in the fixes that you do!"

They pulled into the drive and the place was completely dark. The gray cedar shingles shone dimly against the night sky. Rita stepped out of the truck and headed for the front door. The old house's silhouette brought to mind images of ghosts and haunted houses, giving her the creeps. Once inside, however, she ran up to her room and flicked on her light. Over in the corner under her bedside table there was a vent. She pulled it out easily and just inside laid a tin can with her money in it. She grabbed it and hurriedly put the vent back in place. Finished, she ran back out to Alberta's truck.

Just before she reached the truck she turned back to look at what had been her home since Mama had married Daddy Joe. There was no mistaking the fear she felt as terrifying memories flashed through her mind. Yet there was something else, a certain kind of excitement—perhaps the thrill of escape. Finally, she and Billy were leaving this wretched place once and for all. If she had her way they would never return.

As they drove Alberta explained to her that Mama had planned on leaving for quite some time, only the opportunity never arose. Mama would not leave unless she was positive that each one of her kids would be relatively safe from Daddy Joe's wickedness. It was sad that it took something as tragic as Betty attempting suicide to motivate Mama. In Rita's mind, the right way would have been to leave Daddy Joe at the first sign of trouble, years ago. And the question remained, why did Mama stay? Why, for five awful years, did she stay with a man who not only beat and tortured her during that time, but her children also? To Rita there was no acceptable explanation. She loved her mother deeply, but could not understand her reasoning and was unable to forgive her for the way she handled things. She often tried to put herself in her mother's position, wanting to justify her mother's actions by admitting that if she were confronted with the same situations she might handle things in the same way. Yet, she knew in her heart she would never fall into the predicament that her mother found herself in. There are lines you just don't cross.

. . .She remembered it was raining that night. The raindrops fell softly against the roof, comforting her. Earlier in the evening she and Billy had been sent to bed for horsing around after Daddy Joe had told them not to. Of course, it really didn't matter what they did; they would have been sent to bed anyway.

Mama was passed out. Betty was taking care of Linda—Betty always took care of the girls when Mama was drunk—and Sally was practicing her spelling with Daddy Joe. Rita remembered clearly that it was hard to get to sleep that evening because it was still light outside. Betty must have gotten the baby to sleep because Rita heard Sally ask her to make some popcorn. About five minutes later Rita could smell the freshly popped corn. She and Billy had been sent to bed without supper, so the aroma was torture. It would have been a lot worse had Betty decided to be mean that night, but she was in a good mood and had smuggled some bread and butter into their rooms earlier.

Later that same night Rita had a dream. It was a good dream about a boy in her class who she was crazy about. His name was Matthew. In the dream Matthew was kissing her; first her face, softly, then her lips, softer still. When the trail of his kisses led to her breast she woke up murmuring the word 'no'. Then her blood went cold as a crack of lightning lit her room enough to outline Daddy Joe's form bent over her. Terror gripped her as she felt his hand hard against her face, smothering her attempt to cry for help.

She kicked and scratched him while she wiggled to free herself. She bit the hand that he held over her mouth until she tasted blood. At the very moment he lifted his hand, she screamed.

"Shut up, you little bitch!" he whispered vehemently as his fist slammed into her face.

Again he tried to cover her mouth with his hand. When that didn't work, he grabbed her pillow and pinned it over her face, smothering her screams.

When she realized that trying to scream was a waste of energy she stopped, hoping if she remained quiet he would take the pillow off her face so she could breathe easier.

When he took enough pressure off the pillow to allow her to take in more air, she started speaking in a normal tone. She knew at first he would not be able to make out what she was saying, to him it probably sounded like a muffled blur of words, but she said it anyway. "I won't let you touch me," she half-cried. She could hardly breathe with the weight of his body covering hers, yet with each breath she continued, "You'll have to kill me. I won't let you touch me."

Over and over again she repeated those words, while she prayed and begged God to give her strength.

"Rita," she heard Billy cry. "What's a-matter?"

Daddy Joe cursed under his breath then snapped, "She's had a bad dream, Billy. She'll be okay now that I'm here. You go on back to sleep."

"I'm scared. I want to stay with Rita. Can I please?" Billy was crying.

"Come here, Billy," Rita ordered tenderly, unconcerned over what Daddy Joe might do. All she knew was that Billy needed her, and that's all she cared about. She held out her arms to him.

Rita rocked Billy in arms that were still shaking with fear, trying to comfort him.

"You listen here, Missy," Daddy Joe threatened as he rose from the bed. "I'll do as I please where you're concerned, No childish threats will stop me. It will just be one less mouth to feed."

11-CAMP

Rita didn't have to see his face to know he was sneering at her. He stood there and watched them from the foot of the bed. After a moment she feared he might change his mind and attack her right in front of Billy. Just as she was about to call out to Mama he turned and left the room.

Tears streaked down her face as she remembered the events of that night which occurred almost three years ago. Daddy Joe never attempted to touch her in that way again. Rita guessed he knew he would have to kill her if he did. Why bother with her when there were easier ways of getting what he wanted.

Just then, Alberta's truck fell into a deep rut. Rita had not even realized they were on a two-track road until the jolt made her aware of it.

"Where are we going?" Rita asked, a bit dazed.

Alberta was concentrating on getting out of the rut and didn't answer her right away. Finally, after rocking the truck back and forth, she drove it out.

"Don't ya know where ya are, child? Ya shore spend enough time here, ya oughta know it like the back of your hand," Alberta chuckled.

When the truck stopped and the doors were opened, Rita knew where they were. The scent of the crisp night air that surrounded her answered her question. They were in the pines, next to Hidden Creek.

"Get that flashlight behind the seat, would ya?" Alberta ordered Rita.

"Hey we're in the pines," Billy managed as he yawned.

"Whatever gave you that idea?" Rita said sarcastically. "What are we doing here?" she asked Alberta.

"This is where you're gonna stay 'til your ma comes for ya."

"We can't stay out here. We'll freeze to death!" Rita said half-hysterically. "We don't even have our coats, Aunt Alberta . . ."

"Hold your britches, girl, and point that flashlight on ahead of ya."

Rita did as Alberta told her and to her surprise there was a small trailer about twenty yards away.

"Wow!" Billy exclaimed before he took off to investigate.

Once inside, Alberta searched her pockets for her Zippo. When she found it she fumbled around in one of the cupboards until she pulled out a candle and lit it. Then she went and lit three oil lamps, two on the wall and one sitting on the table. Rita followed her outside so she could show her how to turn on the propane for the stove, which they would be using not only for cooking but also as a heat source.

"I'm not shore when your ma is gonna come for ya. I pray it be soon. If ya need something real bad, like gas or something, don't ya be afraid to call me, ya hear. But if ya don't need anything ya just be still and wait for your ma!"

Alberta left. As she started to drive away Rita glanced at Billy and noticed that he had tears streaming down his face.

"What's the matter, Billy?" she asked as she wrapped her arms around him. She could not imagine what could be bothering him. As for her, for the first time in years she felt somewhat at ease. "We're finally away from Daddy Joe," she said in an attempt to console him. She took in their surroundings. Mama must have been preparing for this for quite some time. Rita noticed many of their personal belongings, clothes, hats and coats. She also saw plenty of food. "Aren't you happy?"

"Yeah. It's just . . . I forgot to tell Mama I love her."

"Don't worry, Billy," Rita said as she held him tighter. "Mama knows."

****

CHAPTER 5

After an hour or so the trailer started to warm up. Billy was his happy self again; his resilience never ceased to amaze Rita. They were putting things away when Billy saw the letter. It was from Mama.

Dear Children,

There are so many things I want to tell you and I just don't know where to begin. Most important, I need you to know how much I love you all, and wish with all my heart I could take back all the pain and suffering you have felt these past years and somehow make things right. I know there is no excuse for my neglectful ways, and yet I need you to know; the death of your father took away my very soul, so selfish was I to let that misery overtake me. I lost my faith in everything, and eventually began drinking. When Joe came to me with the proposal of marriage, he offered support and seemed to be a decent man. I could never have been more wrong about anything, and for that I am devastatingly sorry.

For the past year I have been fighting alcoholism. The less I drank, the more I began to realize the wickedness of the evil man I married. So many times I just wanted to give up. Yet during the darkest times my children kept me going. Even when I was at my lowest, my children stood by me unconditionally. Though I am undeserving of your loving kindness, I accept it, for it's the very fuel that makes me strong. Without it I would be an empty shell of a woman unable to live.

Now I must tell you of a hope that seems too good to be true. Your father may still be alive. I believe in my heart that he is, and I am determined to find him. My faith having been restored leads me now to find your father, the only man I have ever loved!

May the Lord watch over you until my return.

LOVE MAMA

Rita read the letter twice, for Billy.

"See, Rita? I told you it wasn't Mama's fault about Daddy Joe. He fooled her! He fooled into thinking he was nice. She was so sad about Papa, she believed him! So she drank to get rid of the pain, and married Daddy Joe to take care of us while she was drunk . . . only it didn't work out like she thought. And then . . . and then it was . . . it was too late!" Billy squealed out after Rita read the letter the second time. "I wish I knew where Mama was so I could tell her I forgive her."

Billy's whole being seemed to be filled with admiration for Mama. As Rita watched him she felt she would be sick. The vile letter filled her with disgust. What was even worse, however, was how easily Billy had accepted it. He was willing to forgive Mama on the basis of the letter. It made Rita ill. "I need some air," she mumbled as she grabbed a jacket and went out into the night.

It was hard to believe that only yesterday she and Billy had waded in the creek like it was a summer day. Now it felt like winter with the clear and cold October night air surrounding her as she walked down by the creek. Her heart was as cold as the night, for when she searched it for forgiveness for Mama there was none to be found. It was difficult for her to think heavily on the subject. On the surface it was easy to put all the blame on Mama, but, Rita knew in her heart she had to take some of responsibility, after all what had she done to stop the madness? A big "nothing."

The moon caused shadows to fall all around her in an eerie

sort of way. After the few minutes it took to get over feeling sorry for herself, she suddenly became aware of the noises of the night. The only sound she was absolutely sure of was the hoot of an owl. After a moment, every sound began to frighten her. Her heart was pounding as she ran back toward the trailer, the echo of her footsteps scaring her further by sounding as if someone was following her. Was someone following her? She was not going to investigate the matter. She decided that she was just letting her imagination run wild.

"Boo!" howled Billy as he jumped out from behind a tree right in front of her.

Rita fell right down to the ground, her heart ready to give from the force of her fright.

"I got you good, Rita," Billy said as he rolled around on the ground laughing his brains out. "You should have seen your face!" he continued laughing, his arms going to his sides, which were probably beginning to hurt from his laughing so hard.

It wasn't long after that Rita began laughing too. It was strange to be laughing. It seemed foreign coming from her. It was almost like she had forgotten how. They laid there, bathed in the October moonlight, laughing outrageously for several minutes.

"I think we are going to be okay here," Rita proclaimed on a more serious note.

"Yeah," Billy said. "Me too."

"Hey, Billy, do you remember the day you and little Timmy Bishop decided to play bullfrog in that trench Papa had just finished digging for Timmy's parents?" Rita asked him as she rolled over on her back to look up at the moon through the tips of the pine trees.

"Yeah, I remember that. Papa was so mad he made us cut a switch. I couldn't sit for a week!"

"Can you blame him? I mean, when he saw Timmy trying to spear you with that pitchfork, I can imagine he was a little upset," she chuckled, remembering clearly that night when Papa returned home.

You should have seen those two boys, Maggie, Papa had said. *Billy down in the trench hopping like a bullfrog while Timmy took shots at him with the pitchfork. And when I asked them what in the world they thought they were doing, Timmy pouts that he was getting himself some frog legs for supper.* Mama, of course, went rushing to Billy's side to make sure he was okay. Luckily, Timmy hadn't put much force behind his shot. "Didn't you guys think of how badly you could've been hurt?"

"Geez, Rita, I was only four. Why would I think of something like that?" Billy answered with a far-off look in his eyes. "Do you remember the time you and Betty were going to oil the road for Papa so his truck wouldn't always get so dusty? You guys took a whole box filled with oil and emptied about twenty-four quarts on the road in front of the driveway. At first Papa was so mad, but after he cooled off a bit, he asked you why you went and did a dumb thing like that, and you told him you was doing like the big trucks did when they came and oiled the road. I swear Papa laughed so hard he almost cried."

For awhile they stayed silent, basking in their memories of Papa. Then Billy turned over on his side, leaned on his elbow and rested his head on his hand. "Rita, would you tell me the fish story?"

"Oh Billy. Come on, don't you ever get tired of hearing it?"

"No. Will ya?" Her little brother pleaded, sweetly.

"Oh all right, you silly goose. When I was about four, Papa took me down to the creek one day and we caught some minnows, shiners. Anyway I begged him to let me keep them. He said we would have to ask Mama, so we took them home. Mama said she guessed it would be all right as long as I kept them outside. I was happy. I just loved those three little fish, and I named them after my favorite girls, Betsy, Tacy and Tib. That night I could hardly sleep, so I got up early and went to see how my new friends were doin'. I thought I had left them safe on the porch in a well cleaned-out paint can, but when I looked at them, I saw a thin layer of ice covering them. It scared me to death to see my poor little fishies looking like they were frozen solid. I ran into the house screaming bloody murder—I thought I'd killed them. Papa finally clamed me down enough to get me to show him what was wrong. He came outside with me and looked down into the can. He told me to go get a cup of hot water and pour it in—'that'll stir 'em up' he said. Then he said I had better get them back into the creek, or they'd die."

"I went and did what he told me. He was right! As soon as the hot water warmed my girls, they started swimming around like crazy. I was so relieved. We set them free right then. Anyway, a couple of years later, sometime in the winter, I went to my friend Debbie Norton's house after school one day. When we got off the bus Debbie saw her kitty, Toby, lying in the middle of her yard, frozen stiff. He was deader than a doornail. He had probably fallen out of the tree, and died sometime in the night. Debbie ran to him crying hysterically. It was so sad. And then there's me, the stupid little idiot that I was, I went and told her not to worry, that I knew exactly how to bring Toby back to life..."

Billy started snickering, knowing the outcome by heart," I can't believe you were so dumb, Rita."

"Well, you better believe it little brother `cause I was. Do you want me to finish the story or what?"

"You know it!"

"We put Toby on the register in the kitchen and then went and watched some TV and forgot all about him. By the time Debbie's mom got home the stink was so bad—of course we grew accustomed to it and didn't even notice, but her mom sure did. Oh, she was stark raving mad. She took me straight home and told Mama that she felt sorry for her, having to put up with such a terrible child. Mama chased her out with the broom for saying that, so I thought that I was in the clear, but when Papa got home boy, did I get it! I got the whipping of my life and lost my best friend, all in one day."

Billy laughed for a moment, then he became very serious. "Rita . . ." His voice cracked as he nervously toyed with a pinecone, "do you suppose Papa could really be alive?"

"I've felt it all along, Billy. You know that."

"What about the body? How do you explain that?" he asked, doubt showing on his face.

"How many times do I have to tell you? It could have been an Eskimo for all we know! The man's face was smashed beyond recognition."

"But Mama identified him!"

"Mama identified Papa's wedding band and his wallet. For all we know, those things could have been taken from Papa and put on a strange dead man to make it look like Papa was dead."

"But why?"

"Now Billy, if I knew that we would be with Papa right now." She stood up and brushed herself off. "We best get back to the trailer and get some sleep. Tomorrow is going to be a big day."

"What do you mean?" Billy asked as he followed close behind her. He eyed her skeptically. "We better not do anything `til we hear from Mama, or at least until we find out what's going on."

"No more waiting for me Billy. I have a feeling Daddy Joe is the answer to all our questions, and tomorrow I intend to do some spying."

As they reached the trailer Billy stopped. "You go on ahead, Rita, I gotta go. I'll be back in a minute," he said before he walked off toward brush.

The old Trotwood trailer was nice and toasty. Whoever owned it took very good care to see that it remained in excellent condition. It had a nice size bed in one end that had a mountain of blankets on top of it. At least she and Billy would be warm. At the other end of the trailer there was a table with two seats that could be converted into a bed if the need arose. For the time being one bed was sufficient. Among the articles Mama had packed, Rita found some long johns. She put them on, then slipped on a nightgown. Just as soon as she was settled into bed Billy threw open the door and let most of the heat out.

"Come on, were you born in a barn or something? Shut the

11-CAMP

door!" Rita complained from under the covers.

"Sorry," Billy mumbled as he softly shut the door. He found some pajamas and put them on. Only when Rita felt Billy safely against her did she dare to fall asleep and even then it was a fitful sleep filled with nightmares of times past.

CHAPTER 6

Rita woke to the wondrous smell of frying bacon. She knew cooking was not one of Billy's favorite things to do, so either he wanted something or he was really hungry. As she sat there watching him, she felt an exhilarating moment of freedom and it moved her to sing.

"Lord I'm one . . ."

Billy turned around from the stove and looked at her like he was trying to solve her the same as he would an algebra problem.

"Morning," he said. His tone was low, as though he was depressed. "We ain't that far away from home."

"Maybe not, but we aren't there," Rita gleefully chirped. She noticed he was unable to look her in the eye. He was upset about something, but what? Eyeing him carefully for a few more moments she tried to fathom what was wrong. When nothing came to mind she put her thoughts to question. "What's a'matter, knucklehead?"

"Happy Birthday," he mumbled. He began to whistle as though nothing was wrong, looking away from her so she would not see the hurt expression on his face.

"Oh shoot!" She forgot to wish him a happy birthday last night when midnight rolled around. Every year on their day at exactly midnight she would wish him a happy birthday—it was tradition. Only this year so many things had happened that it completely slipped her mind.

Given that Billy was born on her sixth birthday Rita had always felt he was her own special gift from God. From the very day he was born it just seemed like he was made for her. She remembered when Mama called her into her bedroom so she could see him for the first time. He had the biggest, whitest hands she had ever seen on a baby. Rita was so afraid she might hurt him somehow that she kept her distance. He was so little and all, but Mama prompted her to come by the bed so she could see him better. When she walked up close to the bed, Mama told her, "Don't be afraid to touch him, honey, he won't break." So she swallowed hard and timidly put her hand next to her baby brother's. His tender little fingers wrapped around her index finger so tight, it amazed her. She just knew right then that he was going to be the best present she ever got. The fact they were born on the same day played a great role in how close they had become. But it went beyond just sharing the same date of birth. Of all the human beings Rita had ever encountered in her life, Billy was her absolute favorite. She could not imagine her world without him. Sometimes they would fight and tease and get on each other's nerves, but Rita could not have special ordered a better kid brother. Billy was her joy.

"Happy birthday, Billy," she said apologetically. "And there's something else I have to tell you."

"What?"

"I love you."

Without looking at her or acknowledging her love, Billy pointed toward the table. Upon it stood a card, apparently from Mama.

"From Mama?" Rita asked.

"Yeah," he answered. "I found it in the ice box." He handed her a plate of eggs, bacon and French toast with jam. "I got something for you too, it's on the table." He handed her a delicious looking plate of food. "I'm going down to the creek. I hope you like breakfast." At the door he turned and gave her a wonderful lopsided grin—Papa's grin—letting her know that all was forgiven.

After she finished eating and cleaning off the table she went to look for her gift. There was a piece of paper next to the card from Mama. It was a poem.

MY BEST FRIEND

I 'member when we talked about baseball and cars and all that stuff
Even though you're just a girl
And I 'member tellin' dreams and tellin' you everything
And never once in all those days
Did I think you'd give my secrets away
Even though you're just a silly girl
I 'member I was afraid
but always somehow you'd show me a way
To make me hold on to my dreams until they came true
And I'll never forget—my very best friend
It's you

Love, Billy

If there was one person in the world who could move her it had to be Billy. He had always been the driving force pushing her to search for something better. Tears welled in her eyes as she thought about all the things they had been through together. She relished the tender moment because she knew it wouldn't be too long before Billy stopped being so sweet and openly affectionate toward her. How vividly she remembered when he used to be like a teddy bear with his little arms outstretched, always around when she needed a hug. Now he only hugged her if it was deemed absolutely necessary, and even then he would complain or roll his eyes. She missed the little boy who used to solicit hugs, and butterfly kisses, who needed tickles and tousles and thousands of stories. She would never forget the tot who hid behind washcloths, and thought you couldn't see him 'cause he couldn't see you. How many times had he begged her to blow kisses into his face just so he could have the thrill of catching his breath. Those days were gone she knew, but the memories were hers to keep, and now she had his poem to cherish too. She read it again, and felt ashamed because for the first time since Billy was born she had completely forgotten his birthday. She did not have a gift for him, not even a homemade card.

She read the card from Mama. It didn't really say much except how she wished she could have been with them on their birthday. At the bottom of the card was a message to read Psalm 77. 'Remember the past for it will give you hope for the future'. Mama underlined the word 'hope'. She also wrote on the card that they should continue to study as though they were still in school, at least four hours a day.

When Rita finished reading the card she got dressed and went out by the creek to wash up, and to say thanks to her kid brother. As she approached him, he looked at her worriedly.

"Did you like it?" he asked quietly while his bright blue eyes sparkled with a hint of pride.

"It's the best!" Rita praised him. "Billy you are so talented, you're going to be famous some day. Did you make that up last night?"

"No. I wrote it this morning while you slept. I heard some noises outside the trailer and couldn't get back to sleep.

Just then, they heard the sound of a vehicle approaching and hit the dirt at the same time. They stayed low to the ground as Billy whispered, "Do you think it's Aunt Alberta?"

"It didn't sound like her truck," Rita pointed out. She lifted her head enough to see the form of a man trying the trailer door, then going inside. She whispered for Billy to run, and just as he was about to, the man called out.

"Rita . . . Billy. Are you here?" his voice boomed.

An unknown emotion swept over Rita as she recognized the man's voice; it was the green-eyed police officer.

"We're down here!" Rita yelled out nervously, her voice shaky with relief.

Billy looked at her like she was that algebra problem, again.

"Remember that officer from last night?" she said as she stood up.

Billy nodded his head in understanding then asked, "What's he doing here?"

"I don't know, but there's only one way to find out." She started walking toward the trailer with a curious kid brother on her heels.

"Hello," the officer said in a deep, rich voice. The way he looked at her made her very conscious of the fact her hair was a mess. Never before had she been so aware of her appearance; there was something about this man that made it matter. Her hands automatically swept through her mop to create some semblance of order to it.

"Well, I can see this is confusing to the both of you so let's start over . . . I'm Nathaniel Rivers."

As he told them his name he gave his hand. Rita grasped it firmly, and it was huge compared to hers. Nathaniel Rivers, she thought, What a nice name. Then it hit her, "Hey, do you know Bucky Rivers?"

His eyes were cold and somewhat frightening, "How did you come by that name?"

"What?" She was not going to tell him every little thing he wanted to know without finding out a few things for herself. "Why does it matter to you? Do you know him? Are you related?" She watched him intently, quite engaged by the play of emotions that swept across his handsome face as he tried to hide his exasperation with her.

"I'm not going to play games," came his vexed reply through clenched teeth. "How do you know Bucky Rivers?"

Rita did not answer him. Instead, she stood there smiling. *Man, he made her nervous.*

"Can we start over by any chance?" Nathan asked, his velvety voice very controlled. "I'm sorry . . . it's just . . . I get a little edgy. I haven't heard my dad's name spoken by anyone in a long time. You caught me off guard when you said it."

"Bucky Rivers is your dad!"

"Yes, he is . . ." His eyes turned a light hue of green, reminding Rita of the color of grass glistening with early morning dew as the sun shines upon it. She could not help but watch his mouth as he talked. How his lips seemed to accentuate every word. It was difficult to concentrate on what he was saying because she kept imagining how it might feel to have his lips touch hers. From his mouth her eyes wandered to his square chin, then down along his neck to rest upon the buckskin poncho that covered his awesome shoulders. Never in her life had she seen a more powerful set of shoulders on any man, except maybe Papa. As the gorgeous rogue continued conversing with Billy, Rita's eyes slowly traveled a path down his solid chest noticing, as her gaze went lower, the magnificence of his thighs outlined by the faded, form fitting Levi's that he wore. He was quite a specimen. He looked wild, from his thick, unruly brown hair, right down to his moccasins. She had never seen him in anything other than a uniform of some sort, so his being dressed as he was seemed definitely more appealing. He looked like the kind of man that she had always imagined Levi's were made for—strong and rugged, appearing as though he could take on the world. As he stood there with his hands resting in his pockets, she caught sight of a silver and turquoise bracelet on his left wrist. She noticed it had something written on it, and squinted her eyes to try and focus more clearly.

"Nathan, that is what it reads," she vaguely heard him say.

Ugh. Had he noticed her staring at him? She couldn't remember having ever been more embarrassed in her entire life than she was at that moment. She could feel the heat rise to her face and knew it was probably a deep shade of red.

"Is that what you prefer to be called?" she asked, unable to look him in the eye.

"Either is fine with me, Nathan or Nathaniel. My dad preferred to call me Nathan . . . he gave the bracelet to me." There was sadness in his voice as he explained about the bracelet. It left, however, as quickly as it had come for when Rita chanced a look at him he was his cool, controlled self again.

"So, we're supposed to stay here and wait for word from Mama?" Billy asked him.

"Yes, that's right. I'll come by when I get the chance and let you two know what's going on."

Rita was completely irate when she spoke. "So what you're saying is that Billy and I have to sit around here waiting for you?" she glared at him as she waited for an answer; she was so tired of waiting.

"It might be a few days, you may stand if you like—maybe get a little shut-eye." Nathan laughed with an amused expression on his face that didn't quite reach his stone-cold eyes. "Give me a break, huh?"

"Ha, ha . . . You are funny, sir. I can see you have quite the sense of humor." Rita remarked dryly. She understood his exasperation with her, but for the life of her she didn't understand her reasons for being so childish about the whole thing. "Let's try for a moment to be serious, shall we? I have always believed my father is alive; Mama knew that, and she knew I would have done anything to help her find him. If she would have been square with me on the subject we could have put our heads together," she argued with great certainty. It might have been the only aspect of her life she was certain about, but she didn't want the seemingly flawless green-eyed stranger to know it. Since his abrupt arrival into her life something about him made her to want to be better and more together than she believed herself to be. She didn't want him to know the scared, highly erratic, emotionally stunted puppet that she saw in herself, so she became someone else. It was easy to be confident and stable when she was playing Stanwyck or Hepburn. She had always been an emotional girl, able to transform even the simplest situation into a dramatic episode and vice versa. To swing from chaotic, to cool and calm was definitely a more difficult feat, but to her it was almost second nature. It was her way of hiding, escaping from things she felt might truly hurt her if it could not be avoided. Her life seemed to be a series of undirected acts, and it was at times like this that she wished that the Big Director in the sky would just yell, "Cut!"

"Okay, okay . . . you win," Nathan said. Let the little waif think him easy. "Let's go into the trailer, put on a pot of coffee and I'll give you the scoop. Under one condition . . . You must tell me how you know my dad. Is that fair enough?"

"That's fair," Rita agreed.

The trailer definitely seemed to be too small for Nathan. He had to keep his large frame bent slightly as he stood up, to keep his head from touching the ceiling. As he and Billy sat down at the table, Rita got a jug of water from the icebox and poured some in the kettle to boil.

"I was introduced to your mother I'd say, oh, about seven years ago," Nathan began. He had a far off look in his eyes and his thumb and index finger rubbed together in a nervous fashion. "Yes, it was seven years ago, right after my eighteenth birthday. Your mother had hired Dad.

"She hired your dad?" Rita asked, confused.

"Yeah, my dad is a P.I. At the time my dad was showing me the ropes, so to speak, of being a private investigator through your mother's case. I can't tell you about the case because I gave your mother my word I wouldn't disclose any information involving it. Do you mind if I smoke?" he asked, reaching into his pocket and producing a pack of Marlboros.

For a moment Rita was tempted to ask him for one. Every once in awhile she would sneak a cigarette from Mama and smoke it at the B.T. It always seemed to calm her nerves. But she didn't want Nathan to get the wrong impression about her, so she decided against asking him.

"Go ahead and smoke if you want," she said.

"As I was saying." Nathan continued. He went on to tell of his first meeting with their mother, and how her particular case moved him to reevaluate his longtime dream of becoming a P.I.

"Why?" Rita wondered aloud.

"I promised your mother I wouldn't discuss it—remember? Anyway, I decided to join the Police Academy in Lansing because I was pretty sure I wouldn't get into the P.I. racket. I figured I'd start out as a civil servant and work my way up, learning the ins and outs of the trade as I went. A few months after I moved to Lansing, Mom called and informed me she thought there might be something wrong with Dad. When I asked her why, she said because she had not heard from him in a couple of weeks. I told her not to worry. Sometimes Dad would not call when he was working on a case such as your mother's where, for example, he would stay hidden for days on end in one particular spot with nothing but a few candy bars and a thermos of coffee to get him by. Speaking of coffee, I think your kettle of water is starting to boil over."

Rita was so spellbound by Nathan's smooth voice that she completely forgot the water she had put on to boil.

"Oh," she said, blushing slightly. "I guess it is."

She got up to tend to the coffee. "How do you like your coffee?" she asked.

"Black, strong and black. The stronger, the better."

She fixed his cup of coffee, placed it before him and then sat back down.

"Thanks," said Nathan, after taking a sip of his steaming cup. "This really hits the spot."

"Continue your story," she just about ordered.

"Well, I told Mom to let me know if Dad contacted her in the next couple of days. If he didn't, I would spend my weekend searching for him. Which is what I ended up doing then and every weekend thereafter, with no luck. It seemed Dad had vanished off the face of the Earth. I figured his disappearance had something to do with your mother's case, but when I raided his office to search for clues I found someone had already been there. Every bit of information my dad had accumulated concerning your mother's case was gone, along with my only source of reaching the one woman who might help me. It has taken me seven long years to find her, only to find out she doesn't know much more about what happened to my dad than I do. She did say that the last time she heard from Dad, about seven years ago, was in a short note he had sent her from somewhere in Arkansas. She said she had misplaced the letter just before she was going to give it to me. If she had taken care to see where it had been mailed from, we would still be in business," he concluded, more than a little disappointed.

"Jonesboro, Arkansas," Rita confessed to him as she pulled the envelope from her pocket. "This is how I came by the name Bucky Rivers."

The look of surprise, then delight, that flashed across Nathan's features as she read the contents of the letter to him, filled her with an irrepressible sense of pride because she held something that seemed to bring much happiness to him. She brought about the dimple in his cheek with a word: Jonesboro. He didn't have to say thanks, or I owe you one; just the way he was looking at her from across the table was reward enough.

"Where is Mama? Did she go to Arkansas?" Rita asked.

"No. She is hiding out," Nathan said.

"Hiding out? She should be in Arkansas looking for Papa!" Rita cried.

"Calm down," Nathan said, his hands motioning for silence. Her dramatics annoyed him a little. He knew from experience it was hard to reason with an individual guided by such intense emotions. "Joe has everyone in town looking for her. If she heads out of town now, he will find out for sure and put a stop to it. She's spending time now looking for leads. I guess once when Joe thought she was passed out, he made a collect call to a Ms. Daphne Rodgers. Your mom seems to think that if your father is alive, and someone wanted to reach him, without actually reaching him, the most logical way to do that would be through Daphne . . ." Nathan stopped, realizing he had said too much.

"Why would that be logical?" Rita asked.

Nathan squirmed uncomfortably as she waited for his answer.

"I can't answer that." He took a long drag of his cigarette and crushed it out in the ashtray. "Billy, could you run out to my car and get me a pack of smokes?"

"Sure," Billy said as he rose to do Nathan's bidding. Billy was a lot smarter than Nathan had guessed. He knew that Nathan's motive was to get rid of him, and Rita wondered what her brother was going to do about it.

When Billy shut the trailer door behind him, Nathan spoke.

"Rita," he began, "for lack of a better way to tell you, I'm just going to be blunt. Your father was having an affair," he said, "with Daphne."

The trailer door swung open and a furious Billy stood in its opening. "Affair? You mean he was with someone besides Mama? You're lyin'."

Rita was too shocked for words. Papa had an affair? No, it couldn't possibly be true. She looked tearfully at Nathan, hoping he would deny it. Instead, he shook his head yes, making it clear that what he said, he believed to be true.

"This is why your mother hired my dad. She suspected your dad was having an affair, and she wanted to be absolutely sure about it. This is the kind of thing that turned me off about the P.I. business—affair cases can get nasty."

"How do you know your dad's disappearance has anything to do with Papa?"

"Well, I'm not absolutely sure, but I'd bet money on it. Dad was working on the case when he disappeared. He had introduced it to me about six weeks earlier. Of course, he used different names, places and circumstance whenever I was involved—your mom wanted it that way. She allowed my dad to show me the ropes through her case, under those conditions. That's why I couldn't find her. I knew she was from the Ann Arbor area, but that's about it. I really didn't have a clue to who she was. It was pure luck that I ran into her at Social Services while I was handing out bulk cheese. She recognized me right off. Of course when I realized who she was I damn near choked on the questions that came flying out of my mouth. I hounded her for weeks to get some answers. I believed she could help put this whole damn thing about Dad to rest, and that is what brings me here." When he finished, his eyes darted nervously back and forth between Rita and Billy. His reason for being nervous escaped him as he fumbled around in his pocket, then spoke in Billy's direction. "You didn't happen to get my smokes while you were out there, did you?"

Billy just shrugged his shoulders nonchalantly.

Gosh, but he's handsome, Rita thought. She could not seem to keep her eyes off him. His emerald eyes were even more beautiful, sparkling with anger. It probably ruffled his feathers a bit knowing that a twelve-year-old bested him. Well, Rita could not just let Billy have all the fun.

"Just because Mama hired your dad to spy on Papa, that doesn't necessarily mean he was having an affair, does it? I mean do you have proof?" she interrogated.

"We'll, no, actually I assumed that he was because well, Dad would have informed your mother had he found out anything on the contrary.

Rita and Billy looked at each other quite satisfied and shook their heads in agreement, before Rita baited, "That's plain foolishness!" she snapped, "You shouldn't go around making accusations like that about decent people when you have no proof. You have some nerve . . . This note I hold in my hand tells me something to the contrary." Rita sat up straight in her seat. "For instance, you say Mama hired your dad because she believed Papa was cheating on her, correct?" She cleared her throat as she unfolded the letter, "Okay, you take this note, which was sent to Mama from your dad, and you analyze it."

"I have reached my destination safely . . ." She began reading aloud, analyzing it as she went. "Destination being Jonesboro, Arkansas. Upon my arrival . . . which according to the postmark would have been sometime before June 23, 1960 . . . I learned of a few discrepancies on the subject of your interest." "And what was the subject of interest? Was Papa having an affair? Correct? So, your dad drops a note to Mama telling her he has learned of a few discrepancies, in other words, what Mama believed to be true was probably false. I know Papa, and he would never have done what you and Mama have so wrongly accused him of, and this letter proves it!"

"Sometimes the truth is hard to take," Nathan said. "I won't argue with you on the matter." He stood up then, forgetting his height, and bumped his head hard against the ceiling of the trailer.

"Damn! That hurt," he cussed and glared at Rita as if it were somehow her fault that he hit his head.

Rita and Billy looked at each other, both trying hard not to laugh at Nathan who was rubbing the top of his head.

"Maybe that will knock some sense into you," Rita said, her words laced with a not-so-nice laughter. "Speaking of the truth being hard to take . . ." she began, "If Papa is alive, whose body did Mama identify? I know who I would guess." Before the words had even left her mouth she regretted them. Sure Nathan had upset her with what he had insinuated about Papa, but it gave her no warrant for the out-and-out evil that her tongue had unleashed. How could she be so cold and unfeeling, to put to words what she had been thinking since Nathan told her about his dad having been missing. "I'm sorry . . ." she stammered, unable to look at Nathan, afraid that she might see disgust or disappointment in his eyes.

"No, it's okay. I've been thinking the same thing myself, except my dad was much smaller than your dad was. The size difference would have been obvious." He resolved. "Only when you said it well, I got an eerie feeling." He searched his pockets and found a pack of smokes, shook a cigarette loose and tried unsuccessfully to light it. He was shaking terribly. Instinctively, Rita reached across the table to steady his hands. She held her hand on his longer than it was necessary for him to light the cigarette. She liked the rough, warm feel of it and didn't want to move her hand away. The sound of the Zippo lid snapping shut brought her out of the trance that touching him had put her in, and prompted her to put her hands together in her lap.

"What if by some bizarre chance it was my Dad's body that your mother identified?" he uttered as he ran a shaky hand through his thick brown hair. "The worst part is, how in the hell are we going to find out? It doesn't make sense, Dad being killed over a routine affair case. I just don't get it! There are too many unanswered questions. Damn! I wish your mother would get back to me on this. She should have some answers."

"How would your mom take it," Rita asked, "if it was your dad?"

"Mom and Dad never really clicked . . . except in bed. I have seven siblings. A family of four boys and four girls, get my drift? Anyway, she's been living with a man since about six months after Dad's disappearance. I doubt highly if she cares one way or the other."

"Oh," Rita said, somewhat embarrassed by Nathan's answer. For reasons unknown to her, a warm fuzzy feeling started in the pit of her belly and worked its way through her body, causing her to feel weak and confused. Something unexplainable was happening to her. If she had not known any better, she would have thought she was falling head over heels for this too tall, ruggedly handsome, beautiful green-eyed stranger who called himself Nathaniel Rivers. She reached across the table and grabbed his empty coffee cup. "Would you care for more?" was her throaty inquiry.

"No, thanks. I best get going. I volunteered at the fire hall tonight, and I have a few other things that I need to take care of beforehand."

They walked Nathan out to his brand-new '67 Mustang. It was sweet. Red exterior with white leather interior, clean as a whistle. Rita eyed it enviously. Nathan must have noticed her.

"Want to take it for a spin?"

"Me?" Rita was shocked. "You would let me drive this?" she said in awe as she lightly touched the polished door handle. "I don't have a license."

"You don't?" Nathan sounded surprised. "You're seventeen, right?" He watched her delicate fingers caress his car, and for a moment he wanted to be his car.

"Eighteen," she corrected.

"Yeah . . . It's our birthday today!" Billy chimed.

"What?"

"I'm 12," Billy said proudly.

"You were born on the same day six years apart? Hmm, that's odd. Well happy birthday to both of you." Nathan seemed to reflect on the information. "Well Rita, if you're 18, why don't you have your driver's license?"

"Daddy Joe was dead set against it. He said I would never have a car to drive anyway. So I never got my license, but I know how to drive." she explained. She figured since Nathan was a police officer he wouldn't let her drive his car after learning she did not have her license. She was wrong.

"Get in, and take her for a spin." he said.

"Can I drive it too?" Billy crooned.

"Sure can little buddy." Nathan smiled and handed Rita the keys. It made her very aware of him, his smile, so much so she had to decline his offer out of shyness.

"Maybe I shouldn't, but please let Billy or he will never forgive me."

"Okay," Nathan's smile faded, "suit yourself."

Two seconds later Billy was behind the wheel with Nathan in the passenger seat.

"Coming?" Nathan asked as he sat back leisurely in the seat and put his hands behind his head.

Rita thought for a moment that he could have easily persuaded her to do anything he wanted with that dream-weaving stare of his. "No, that's okay." She murmured as she walked slowly and deliberately around to his side of the car. She leaned over his door and boldly picked his pack of cigarettes out of his pocket, shook one loose and offered it to him while commenting sweetly. "I think I would be too nervous knowing Billy has never driven a day in his entire life." She was teasing, but her eyes were serious and never faltered from his. Her breath was warm and enticing, and her sweet lips were just mere inches away.

It was an intense moment for Nathan, and a pent-up sigh escaped him, "Hmmm . . ." He was surprised by the effect the girl had on him.

He seemed a little uneasy so Rita added, "Don't worry, I'm sure with your expert assistance Billy will do just fine." Then she winked at him. "Good luck," she said to Billy. Then she watched them drive slowly away. She had the sinking feeling she was going to miss out on more than just a simple ride.

About twenty minutes later she heard the sound of an engine purring outside the trailer. She looked out the window to see Billy shaking hands with Nathan and thanking him profusely. Then Nathan drove away. Simple words could not explain how sad she felt when this happened. For some reason she had it in her head that he would come back inside the trailer and stay awhile. Billy barged in filled with excitement, his mouth chatting at full speed.

"Man, you should have seen me, Rita, I did great! Nathan said I was a very good driver, and he promised me that when he had more time he'd let me drive again. He said he'd like to take you and me cruisin' down Telegraph sometime. He said we might even see a drag race! I never have seen a real one—I saw one in a movie." Billy breathed, quite fascinated by it all "Anyway, he said he'd come back as soon as he could, hopefully with news from Mama. Oh, and here." A very excited Billy pushed a grocery sack into his sister's hands.

"That's great Billy! I am happy for you. You've had a nice drive in a sharp car, but right now we have other things to worry about! Okay!" Rita snapped. She wished now that she would have gone for the drive. "What is this?"

"Open it, knucklehead."

Rita opened the sack and couldn't believe her eyes. She laughed heartily and shook her head in disbelief for the darn thing was stocked full of beef jerky and Slim Jims. "Goodness Billy . . .what in the world? Where did you get all these?"

"Well, we went down to Crider's Corner, Spag's Grocery, and then to the drugstore. Nathan asked me what I thought you'd like for your birthday—I told him jerky was your favorite thing." Billy just beamed. "You know what? I think he likes you. You like him, don't you? You act real funny around him. You ought to just be yourself, Rita; 'course I like you no matter what you act like," he finished, while giving her his sweetest puppy-dog eyes.

Rita hated that Billy knew her so well. What was it about

Nathan that had attracted her? The fact he was gorgeous might have something to do with it, but she had never put much stock in looks. She learned early in life that the most beautifully wrapped presents were often nothing more than an empty box. Therefore, with Nathan it was more than looks; it went beyond that. Maybe it was fate. Or maybe it had something to do with the fact he was the kind of guy who would go buy her a sack of jerky just because he knew it was her favorite. She smiled to herself at the thought.

"All right, Billy, we've talked enough about Nathan. As far as I'm concerned, it's a closed subject. Right now we have more important things to be worried about, like finding Papa. Agree?"

"Agree. You're the boss, but I don't know why?"

"Hey, what happened to my sweet and innocent kid brother? You're acting as if you're twelve going on thirty-five. I'd say it would be best if you concerned yourself with things that your twelve-year-old mind can comprehend and let me worry about the rest."

"Aye, aye, captain," Billy saluted. He was having problems keeping a straight face.

"Billy, let's be serious. Now we've got to go to the house and try to get some information. Hopefully Daddy Joe is gone, and the house is empty. If so, I'll be going inside to look for clues. You will keep a lookout. Climb the old willow tree and make sure you warn me if Daddy Joe comes. When you spot him, climb down and hide yourself. Whistle that ear-piercing whistle of yours, and make sure you give me enough time to get to safety. Okay?"

"I don't think we oughta? Shouldn't we wait? What if Daddy Joe catches us? He'll kill us!" Billy yelled as he fidgeted nervously at the trailer door while Rita walked off toward the pines.

"You can stay here if you like, Billy. I'm going to the house and that's all there is to it, with or without you," she lied, hoping Billy would take the bait. He did, and she felt much better when she heard his soft footsteps fall into place behind her.

****

CHAPTER 7

Daddy Joe's car was not parked in the driveway when they arrived at the house so they assumed he was not home. Before Rita went into the house she made sure Billy was in place up in the willow tree. Only then did she go about her business.

The place looked like a pigsty, with beer bottles scattered all over the floor, some being half full. There were stains on the wall where it looked like someone smashed a beer bottle against it. A smelly, stinking mess, just like Daddy Joe. The whole scene made Rita shiver at its familiarity. She walked up the stairs being careful not to step on the broken glass that lay scattered on the steps. There was creak in the floor that sounded unmistakably like someone was walking down the hall upstairs.

Rita ducked at the sound, then slowly retreated back down the steps, scarcely breathing. She kept her eyes peeled to the top of the stairs, but saw nothing. As she approached the bottom step, she turned her gaze away from the top of the stairs to search for an escape.

"I see you sneakin' around, you dirty rotten . . ." Daddy Joe's slurred speech came from the top of the stairs.

Sheer terror paralyzed her as she recognized who spoke the almost inaudible words. So slurred was his speech from being drunk, that it sounded as if he were speaking in a foreign language. Then he fell. His twisted body made gruesome thumping sounds as it hit each step, until finally he came to a halt right beside her.

He lay there, at the foot of the stairs, unmoving. Except for labored rise and fall of his chest, he looked as though he were dead. She watched him carefully for a moment, and contemplated whether to flee or resume the duties of her original plans. When Daddy Joe began to snore, the decision was made easy for her.

Slowly, she climbed over him, then continued quietly up the steps. When she reached the room that Mama and Daddy Joe had shared, she searched frantically for anything that might give her a clue to Papa's whereabouts.

Throughout the time she had lived in Daddy Joe's run-down hundred-year-old farmhouse, rarely had Rita attempted to step foot inside the room that he and Mama had shared. She was not supposed to enter it under any circumstances. When she reached the corner of the room where the red velvet drapes hung, she pulled them back and saw the telephone. It reminded her of one time that she had dared to set foot in the room.

. . .Daddy Joe and Mama had gone out that night with Sheriff Vanderpool and his wife. They were going to celebrate Daddy Joe's birthday by having a surprise party for him at Millie's restaurant. Rick was living at home at the time, so automatically he became the sitter for the night.

Basically they could do whatever they wanted to when Rick was in charge, under the condition that Daddy would not find out about it. Many times when Mama and Daddy Joe were out, Bobby and Timmy Bishop would cruise over on their mini-bikes and let everyone take turns riding them down by old Mister Zeeb's gravel pit.

The night of Daddy Joe's birthday, however, Rita was not up to the usual. She had decided to stay in the house. She had an uneasy feeling that something bad was going to happen and could not shake it.

The tube was tuned to the *Lawrence Welk Show* as she situated herself on the davenport, trying to get comfortable, when the faint sound of the telephone ringing upstairs caught her attention. She ran up the stairs to answer it, but stopped short of the room. She knew she was not supposed to touch the phone, but it kept ringing.

Overcoming her fear, she opened the door and peeked inside. The light from the hall cascaded through the room and came to rest on the red velvet drapes. From behind those drapes the phone kept ringing, seeming to be more urgent. She ran to the drapes and pulled them back, and there on the lonely bay window seat sat the urgently ringing telephone. Rita picked it up.

The voice on the line whispered, yet it was frantic in its intensity. "Mrs. Klein . . . Mrs. Klein. Are you there? Help us, please!"

"Who is this?" Rita stammered, frightened by the alarm in the strange man's voice.

"Bucky Rivers . . . get us to hell out of here . . ."

Then a dial tone.

The memory sent chills down Rita's spine. *This is crazy!* She thought. Once again her stubbornness had put her and Billy both into a compromising position. What do I expect to do against Daddy Joe if he has a mind to kill me? This thought propelled her to act quickly. She ran down the hall then took the stairs three at a time, jumping over Daddy Joe as she did so.

She ran out of the house. Billy saw her and quickly climbed down the willow. She kept running and he met up with her in the thickness of the pines.

"What happened? Did you find something?"

"Daddy Joe was home so I had to get out of there."

Billy looked as if he might swallow his tongue. "What do you mean, Daddy Joe's home? Where's his car, then?" He howled, unbelieving.

"I don't know where his car is, but I'm telling you, he was home! And drunker than I've ever seen him. He saw me, but I'll bet he won't remember it by morning. He'll be sporting a headache from more than a hangover tomorrow."

As they walked, Rita thought about her strange memory. It confirmed to her that the mangled body discovered in Alaska was definitely not Bucky Rivers. She could hardly wait to divulge the news to Nathan. She contemplated whether to tell Billy, but decided against it. Maybe the less he knew the better, since she had already endangered him far more than was intended.

Three cold uneventful nights passed as November rolled in, bringing snow. Billy had been disappointed because he missed out on trick or treating, so to appease him Rita gave him most of her Slim Jims and promised to take him to Millie's to get a sundae as soon as she could. They spent a lot of time huddled together in the corner of the trailer playing hangman and tic tac toe until their fingers got cold. At that point they would take turns telling stories or making up songs that would someday, no doubt, make them famous. They had run out of propane the day before. Stuck with only three oil lamps, they put them together to generate enough heat to keep from getting frostbite. Then they constructed a teepee out of a blanket, making the best of what resources they had. For one whole day they sat around the oil lamps as if it were a bonfire. After four full days without word from anyone, Nathan came.

They had just finished eating beans and jerky, when the trailer door swung open. Standing in the entry was Nathan with a propane tank in one hand and a pack of batteries in the other. He looked very much like what Rita had imagined a pioneer would look like. He would never know the effects the mere sight of him had on her heart, for she herself could not explain it.

Billy jumped out from under the teepee. "It's good to see you, Nathan. I was getting worried that something might have happened to you. Some'm real bad. What took you so long?" he asked.

"It's a long story, Billy," Nathan replied. "It's cold in here, what happened? Did you run out of gas?" he asked.

"No," Rita said saucily. "We shut off the heat because we like it this cold in here."

Nathan smiled a wonderfully wicked smile in her direction. "I missed you too, Rita."

Before she could reply he grabbed the full propane tank and headed back out the door.

Within minutes he was back inside the trailer. He turned all four burners on the stove to the high position, then lit them simultaneously with one match. Of course this was a magical feat in Billy's eyes, another talent of Nathan's that fascinated Rita's simple little brother.

This made Rita jealous. Never in her life did she have to compete with anyone, except Mama, for Billy's attention, until Nathan came along. She had to admit, it wasn't settling too well with her.

"Got some coffee?" Nathan asked, his words clipped by his chattering teeth.

He stood there, shivering from the cold, looking irresistibly charming. In that moment she forgot what it was that she resented and set out to make some coffee.

"Have you heard from Mama?" she asked.

"As a matter of fact, she's the reason I haven't been out here. I've been to Arkansas and back this week."

"What?" came Billy's cry of disbelief. "Didn't she want to come and see us before she went all the way to Arkansas?" he whined as tears welled in his eyes.

It was obvious that Billy missed Mama desperately. It was upsetting that Mama could be so driven and uncaring of Billy's feelings not to take a few hours to come and see him before she continued her quest to find Papa. Billy tried to hide his tears. He did not want Nathan to think he was a baby. But Rita knew his little heart was breaking inside. It made her wish that she could comfort him, hug him or something. But that was definitely a no-no in Nathan's presence.

Within the hour the trailer was warm and toasty again. Nathan apologized for the fact they had run out of propane. He thought they should have had enough gas to last four or five days at least, that is, if it was used wisely.

Rita watched him as he talked, the way his large hands moved in harmony with his words when he was trying to get his point across. A few times he noticed she was staring and matched her stare with his own. The chill she felt less than an hour ago could not be remembered as the intensity of his stare warmed her.

Rita had acquired a few boyfriends since junior high. Most of her relationships had lasted a day or two, or at most a week given how things were at home. Yet they were just boys; Nathan was definitely a man. Having never been in a romantic relationship with a man, the emotions she was experiencing now were new and wonderful, yet scary to say the least.

What was he thinking when he looked at her with those piercing green eyes of his? This man, who came into her life less than a week ago, turning her world upside down, breaking through the wall she had so carefully built with his wholesome honest-to-goodness nature and his steady probing gaze. She had despised most of the men she had been acquainted with throughout her life, with the exception of Grandpa Klein and Papa. So, how was it that this state trooper sitting across from her had entwined his way so easily into the fibers of her very soul? She did not know. What she did know was that if she was not careful, the wall she had built to protect herself would come crashing down to expose her to the kind of hurt Mama felt when she thought she had lost Papa. That, Rita was sure, would bring her to her knees.

"Rita, will you come outside with me?" Nathan requested. "I need your help. Billy, I'm going to need you to keep an eye on this stove. Let me know if it goes out," he instructed Billy, then helped Rita with her coat.

Once outside, they walked silently to where the propane tank was hooked up, and before Rita knew what was happening Nathan brought her to him in his strong embrace. He held her off the ground to where her head rested in the crook of his neck and his lips rested against her ear.

"Do you know what you do to me?" he whispered softly, "when you look at me the way you do?"

Then he kissed her, gently, exploring her mouth with his tongue. The feeling he created within her could only be defined as hunger, and Nathan is what she hungered for. She began to kiss him back, urgently, trying to bury herself in him.

Nathan was trembling when he lifted her away from him. The

way he looked at her made her want to tell him right then and there that she was madly in love with him; instead she backed away, still tingling in the places where his hands had been holding her, embarrassed by her wanton reaction to his kisses.

As if he read her thoughts, he pulled her into his arms again and held her close to him. "Girl, you are adorable." He laughed. "You're quite engaging," he said, as he looked down at her with eyes shining brightly as if they were beholding a treasure or something. "The trip to Arkansas with your mom was difficult because every time I looked at her, I saw your face, and your beautiful brown eyes. Did you know that you look a lot like your Mom?"

"I look more like Papa," Rita said. She began to feel very awkward, due to his compliments, like a silly schoolgirl unsure how to act. "Why do you like me?" she wondered aloud as it struck her as unbelievable that a man such as himself could be the slightest bit interested in her.

"What do you mean, why?" He seemed confused. "Why do I like you? Hmm, that's a hard one," he teased, then he became serious. "When I first saw you," he explained, "laying in the grass the day you and Betty went to the hospital. You looked up at me with those eyes of yours and I felt something, something that made me wish to know you. I don't even think you were aware of what you had done. You're a cute kid, that's for damn sure."

She blushed at the thought.

"Still," Nathan continued, "you're very pretty, but . . . " He looked at her appreciatively. "But that is not all of what I find interesting about you—you intrigue me. I guess what I'm trying to say is I would like to get to know you." He finished, as his thumb and index finger went at it in a nervous fashion again.

"Nathan," Rita started hesitantly, "I just don't know. I'm afraid." Her words seemed to make him tense.

"Damn, Rita, that's the last thing I want you to be. I don't want you to be afraid of me. I don't want you to be afraid of anything, anymore. I've told you how I feel. Take as long as you want to think it over, and when you decide how you feel about us, clue me in. I'll wait." He pulled away again, putting distance between them. "I've been trying to keep quiet on the way I feel about you because of everything that's going on right now. Under normal circumstances, I would have first asked you out, and then taken you to a nice place for dinner and maybe a movie. But, now, our lives are far from normal. I can't explain why I feel the way I do about you. I just like passing the time with you. With you, minutes don't seem to be so painfully long."

"Don't misunderstand me, Nathan," Rita pleaded. "I'm not afraid of you. I'm just not ready to be involved. I need to straighten out my life. If I get wrapped up with you now, I would always feel like I've burdened you with my problems and that wouldn't be fair."

"Why can't I help you with your problems?" he offered.

"Because you don't even know me," she cried. "Believe me, you can't even imagine how I perceive this thing called life. Most of the time I just want to end it. Now be honest with me, would you really like to deal with a psychopath for the rest of your life."

He was angry, that was obvious. "You're a far cry from being a psychopath; trust me, in my line of work I have dealt with a few. The problem is why do you think you're one? Because of the things that son-of-a-bitch did to you? He's the psychopath! For all you've been through, I think you're one of the most levelheaded people I know. I also know you're pretty damn stubborn, and if you think you're psycho, there's not much I can do to change your mind. It's hard for me to stand here and listen to you knock yourself!" he snapped, and with that he turned and left her standing alone. Uncaring of the bitter cold outside she began to walk, unaware of her destination, she just needed to get away.

A fierce anger surged through Nathan as he struggled to control his thoughts of revenge against Joe Welch. The crisp November air worked to cool him down, and after a moment he began to think clearly again. He saw in his mind repeated images of Rita being hurt by Joe. He needed to exercise the rage he felt toward the man for having touched Rita. He knew there was only one way, and he intended to follow through if given the chance. How could anyone do the things he had heard Joe did to Rita and her brothers and sisters? In his line of work he had seen this sort of thing several times, only it never seemed to reach him as this did. He vowed he would do everything in his power to protect Rita and Billy from ever being hurt again, by anyone, let alone Joe. They were damn good kids. Rita was more than good, she was lovely.

****

When Rita returned to the trailer, she stood outside the door momentarily. She could hear Billy talking to Nathan so she decided to eavesdrop on their conversation.

"I haven't told Rita about it yet," Billy was saying, "but I've had the same dream three times since we've been staying here at the trailer. Every time it starts out just the same. I'm packed in this convertible and hundreds of people fit in it, just hundreds and hundreds of people. And all the people in it are strangers to me, except for one, Timmy Bishop."

"Who?" Nathan asked.

"Timmy Bishop. He was my best friend. Timmy and I always hung out together when we were little. One day, Timmy and me were walking along the road looking for bottles to take back to the store for spending money. I thought I saw a bottle down in a ravine and went to check it out. While I was down in the brush I heard a car coming. Two seconds later I heard an awful thud and then the car sped away. I knew Timmy had been hit. I don't know how I knew I just did. I ran up the ravine to help my buddy, but I couldn't find him. Then I saw what looked like a doll by the side of the road, all broken up and bloodied. I knew without even being near him that he was dead. There was nothing I could do but cover his face with my jacket. Whoever hit him didn't even care to see if Timmy was dead or not. He just left him on the side of the road like he was road kill or something."

Rita listened intently as Billy told Nathan about Timmy. Billy had never spoken to anyone, except the police, about Timmy Bishop's death, not even her.

"Well, anyway," Billy continued to tell Nathan about the dream. "I'm in this gigantic car with all these strangers and Timmy. Only Timmy acted like he didn't even recognize me. I started to put my hand on his shoulder to tell him who I was, but my hand sunk right through his body. By this time I was scared silly. I wanted to scream, but my voice wasn't working right. I started to yell out for help, but nothing came out. And Nathan, it seemed so real. I looked out of this huge car and there are all kinds of people lining the side of the road. In the dream I'm crying and waving to Mama and Rita and the rest of the family. They're all standing by the edge of the road doing the same, and saying good-bye to me. Then the car slowly drives away, and I wake up. I think this is God's way of telling me He's going to take me to Heaven soon . . ." then he paused for a moment as if debating what to say next. "I'm really worried about Rita and what she's going to do once I'm gone. So if you'd just give me your word that you'll look after her, I sure would feel better."

Concern for Billy filled Rita as she listened to his interpretation of the dream. She could only imagine how worried her poor kid brother had been these last few days awaiting his so-called foretold death. Why hadn't he confided in her about the dream? Did he think that he was protecting her? Was he saving her from worry? Or had they lost their ability to communicate as they had so easily before. It saddened her to think so; she prayed that was not the case. It was consoling to know Billy seemed able to confide in Nathan, yet as she secretly listened to them she felt a tinge of envy.

"Timothy Bishop, you say?" Nathan mused. "I remember that tragic accident. It happened on Old 23, just after the real sharp curve, didn't it?"

"Yeah," Billy whispered.

"That was pretty terrible all the way around," Nathan commented. " It was a no-win situation."

"What do you mean?" Billy asked.

"We'll, the way I remember it is a little different than what you have described to me. A girl, Sheila something-or-other, reported the accident over the telephone. She was a teenage counselor who spent the better part of her summer working at that youth camp. What was it?"

"The Little Brook Ranch?" said Billy.

"Yes, that's the one. The Little Brook Ranch. The girl was hysterical when she called. The dispatcher could barely understand her and had to ask her to repeat herself several times. The dispatcher finally found out the girl believed she might have hit a small child on Old 23 and would someone please hurry out to the location and check around. The girl went on to explain she would be at the emergency clinic at the county hospital, where she had rushed three kids from the camp because they had eaten poisonous flowers. She kept saying over and over that she didn't know what to do. She said she wasn't absolutely sure she had hit a person, but was sure she hit something of small stature."

Rita felt sorrowful as she continued to eavesdrop. How awful it seemed to her the predicament had been for that girl, having to make that split-second decision with human lives in the balance.

"Come in, Rita!" she heard Billy call.

She was caught for the spy that she was. Slowly she opened the door, ashamed that she had been secretly listening in the first place. But she didn't give them a chance to harass her about it before she asked Nathan, "What happened to the other kids, the ones who ate the flowers? And the girl, what happened to her?"

"The three kids from the camp were saved. Timothy, as you both well know, was killed instantly from the impact of the car. Sheila was charged with negligent homicide, but the prosecutor's office, along with Mr. and Mrs. Bishop, decided to drop the charges against her.

Isn't it strange, Billy," Nathan suggested, "to find out that something you have believed to be true for the last few years is actually far from the truth in reality? I hope I haven't upset you in any way, I only meant to set you straight."

"That is weird," Billy breathed. "All this time I pictured some drunk and mean-looking man had done it, someone who looked like Daddy Joe. Wait a minute that's right! I remember now, the guy, the policeman said something to me about a girl, but at the time I wasn't thinking clearly. That is so strange." Then Billy looked in Rita's direction. "What about my dream? What, do you think, Rita?"

"That was quite a dream, Billy. But the fact you think the dream is the Lord's way of speaking to you beats anything I've ever imagined by far. I think you've been under a lot of stress lately and the dream is your mind's way of dealing with it."

"I believe your sister has made a very good observation of the situation," Nathan said with a velvety drawl as he stood up, being careful of his height, and reached for his coat.

"Where are you going?" asked Billy.

"I've got a long walk ahead of me. I better get started now if I want to make it to my car before dark."

"Where's your car?" Rita asked.

"I parked it in town because I'm driving the Falcon and I don't have chains on the tires. I knew without the chains the Falcon wouldn't have a chance on these trails, so I just walked from town. I should get going now."

"Can't you stay here?" Billy practically begged.

Rita had to admit that she wanted Nathan to stay just as much as Billy did, possibly more, but she was not about to let Nathan know it, not after the way he treated her. Only when he glanced her way as if he were looking for her permission or something, she didn't know what to do.

"Would you?" The plea was out of her traitorous mouth before she could help herself.

Nathan smiled. "You want me to stay?"

"No," she pouted. At this point she was putty in his hands.

Nathan laughed lightheartedly then put his coat down on the

bench table seat. "I'll stay tonight," he announced. "Tomorrow, I'm taking you both to my mom's, where I know you'll be safe."

As Rita listened to Nathan she believed his words were true. He would keep them safe. Just his presence made her feel more relaxed and safe than she had felt in years. She had a wonderful time just listening to him and Billy converse. The lull of Nathan's voice along with the feeling of peace she felt from his presence was just what she needed to feel good again; to feel good enough to dream about starting over, somewhere far away from Daddy Joe.

"Have you thought about school? As far as when and where Billy will attend?" Nathan asked from out of the blue. "You know this might drag on for months."

Rita had been daydreaming about renting an apartment somewhere in a small town, and having Mama and Papa over for coffee and cake, when Nathan posed the startling question.

"Actually, I hadn't even thought about it."

"I don't need to go to school! I'm not going to be around very much longer, anyhow!" Billy piped in.

"Billy! I don't want you talking that nonsense anymore!" Rita scolded, then directed her attention toward Nathan. "There is someone I know who could teach Billy without him actually having to go to school."

"Who?" Both Billy and Nathan asked.

"Olivia Welch. Daddy Joe's sister-in-law."

"Are you kidding me?" Nathan asked incredulously.

"No, I am not kidding. Mrs. Olivia Welch is one of the kindest women I have ever had the pleasure of knowing. She dislikes Daddy Joe immensely and would probably enjoy spiting him. I'm sure she would love to help us by either teaching Billy or supplying us with the materials we would need for Billy to study at home."

Nathan raised an eyebrow at that. "What home?" he asked.

"We'll," Rita stammered, "I have close to nine hundred dollars, which should be enough to set us up in an apartment and get us by for a month or so."

"Yes, but what happens when the money runs out? What will you do then? I don't mean to rip the pages of your fairy tale or anything, Rita, but it's a rough and tumble world out there, and ah, you may not be able to get by on your looks alone. Even though you are a fine-looking young woman," Nathan added, with an anything but innocent twinkle playing in his eyes.

Rita blushed at his somewhat twisted compliment, then quickly regained her composure. "I planned on getting a job!" Nathan's questioning suddenly irritated her.

"Where?" he shot.

"When you saw Mama did you hear anything about Betty? And Linda and Sally, how are they? Do you know anything concerning them?"

He looked at her warily, yet resigned himself to her line of questioning, figuring it would boost her confidence. He liked her tactics, not to mention her spirit. "Betty will be going home with Alberta this Monday. She'll be required to get some counseling until she's considered "well." As for Sally and Linda, they're staying at your grandparents' place. Before we left for Arkansas your mom needed to talk with your grandma so we stopped there. Your grandma said Joe had been by several times, and always she would act sympathetic to his cause by telling him she would look after the girls until he could get this whole mess straightened out. If there is one thing I have learned about the women in your family, it would be their unmatched ability to lie outright and not even blink an eye about it."

Rita didn't know whether to take that statement as a put-down or a compliment. She acted humorously outraged by it and warned, "Listen here Nathan, you're way off track. We have only lied to protect family. If you don't apologize, I might have to slap you. I won't have you talking about my family like that!" She had a hard time containing the smile that threatened to spread across her face, and she almost choked on the laughter that welled inside her as she watched Billy look on nervously. Nathan was at least three times Billy's size, and although they were no match, she had no doubt her kid brother would have called Nathan out if he had done anything other than apologize.

"Sorry." Nathan obliged.

Rita smiled warmly.

Nathan loved to see her smile. She always hesitated a little at first, her eyes remaining serious, but with a little work he would end that. Then with lightning-quick speed his hand snaked out across the space between them and he grabbed her arm and held it with an iron grip. "What happened there?" he asked, pointing to the jagged scar on the crook of her left arm.

Rita started to get light-headed as she remembered the events that led to the appearance of the unsightly scar. She felt a tightening in her chest and pleaded, "I need some air," as she staggered to the door. Nathan still held her arm, except now it seemed more for support than anything else.

"Are you okay?" he whispered, concern filling his velvety-lined voice. "Did I frighten you?" he asked, his eyes laden with distress.

She wanted with all her heart to tell him no, but the word would not come. After a few big gulps of air, she was able to breathe normally. She closed the door and Nathan helped her to the table seat. She felt like crying as she looked at the two of them, Billy and Nathan, with worry etched in their brows. Then Billy spoke.

"I remember that day," he said quite distressed. "You and me were gonna go down to the creek, but Mama hollered from the window that we was to get the laundry hung out to dry before we did anything else. `Course we knew better than to complain. I remember you said, 'Last one to the clothesline has to do most of the hanging!' and you let me win—you always let me win. We only had a little left, and I took over for you `cause you decided to put on an acrobat show for me . . ."

As Rita listened to Billy it all came back to her, as clear as if it had been the day it happened. "Ladies and gentleman," she had said, drawing it out like a circus announcer. "Introducing to you for the first time anywhere, the most amazing trapeze act you'll ever witness, to be performed today by the Great and Reckless

Rita!" She had acted like a circus performer that day not so long ago for Billy. She lifted herself easily up the old iron clothesline pole. "A hush falls over the crowd as Reckless Rita begins her death-defying act." She did some tricks she had learned to do on the monkey bars at school, only there were no big iron hooks on the school monkey bars and before she knew it, the sharp iron hook poked through the inside of her left arm like it was Jell-O. And there she was, hanging by the crook of her arm. She tried to pull herself off the hook with her free arm. It took every ounce of energy she had to attempt it, but there was no way she could maneuver it. At first Billy thought it was part of her act, but it only took him a moment to realize it was no act and she was in dire need of assistance. He then came rushing to her aid.

"You get from there, boy!" Daddy Joe viciously shouted from the inside the shed. He walked slowly toward them, a crude smile spread across his wicked face. "How many times do you have to be told not to horse around when you're s'posed to be doing your chores?" he asked, while his black eyes gleamed with hostility. "We'll, Missy, looks like you got yourself into one hell of a fix now." He pushed her then, causing her body to swing back and forth, which in turn caused a sharp agonizing pain to pierce from her arm to her shoulder. She remember how awfully bad she had wanted to scream when Daddy Joe continued to push her back and forth, but she couldn't, not without further frightening an already scared to death Billy, who stood motionless, fear paralyzing him.

"You're such a smart ass!" Daddy Joe's wicked tongue lashed, while his eyes brimmed with hate. "You figure out how to get out of this one." Then he threw back his head and laughed an evil, sinister laugh.

Rita remembered it was so hot that day she had been drenched with sweat. It made it even harder to attempt to get a grip so that she might pull herself off the hook. After each unsuccessful try she would be completely exhausted. To rest, she would have to hang with all her weight pulling her toward the ground, the force of her weight tearing her flesh where she was hooked. She was frightened, yet somewhat fascinated by the blood streaming down her arm. She tried to be brave for Billy's sake, even though the pain was almost unbearable.

Billy started crying, murmuring "I'm sorry . . . I'm sorry" over and over again.

"Billy!" she screamed, unafraid of Daddy Joe at this point. "Come here!"

"Shut up, girl!" Daddy Joe spit the words out, scaring Billy into stopping short of where she was impaled.

"God, I'm going to die like this!" she cried out in agony, hoping that God Himself would hear her plea and save her from further torture.

All of a sudden Billy fell to his knees under her, clasped his little hands together, looked up toward the heavens and began to pray. His voice was high-pitched either because he wanted to drown out anything said by Daddy Joe or he was hysterical, Rita could not tell which.

"Dear God," he prayed, "please help Rita." His eyes were squeezed closed. "Please."

While Billy prayed a warmth came over Rita, a calming warmth, the kind she used to feel when Papa would kiss her goodnight. It made her strong, this warmth, so that she could wrench herself off the hook. It helped that Billy was just close enough for her to reach with her feet and use for leverage.

When Billy opened his eyes she was lying on the ground next to the clothesline pole.

Daddy Joe just shook his head in disgust and walked back toward the shed. That in itself was enough to make Rita believe Billy's prayer was heard and answered. She whispered her thanks to the Lord and with Billy's help went cautiously into the house to clean the wound. They did not want Mama to find out because it would have given her an excuse to have another beer. They were not about to be the cause of her drinking. After pressing a cold cloth to the area for several minutes, the bleeding stopped. They wrapped it with a clean rag. Ironically, they used a scrap piece of clothesline to secure the rag over the wound.

"And after God answered my prayer, we went and cleaned off the blood and stuff. There was a hole in her arm over an inch deep, but she never even went to Doc Bailey's. She never even told Mama about it!"

Nathan unexpectedly bent his head and kissed the jagged white. He wanted to take on all her hurts. As he pictured the scene with his mind's eye, he felt the rage again, but held his emotions in check.

Billy rolled his eyes, then finished his story. "Betty must have been watching 'cause after that day she always volunteered to hang the clothes whenever Mama wasn't in the mood to do it herself. That left me and Rita off the hook."

"Nice choice of words, baby brother!" Rita hailed.

Billy laughed nervously until he "got it" and then he really started to snort and snicker. It was good to be able to laugh carelessly; it was even better to watch Billy do it.

Suddenly Nathan put a finger up to his mouth, motioning for them to keep quiet as he pressed his ear against the door. "Someone's out there!" he hissed. "Damn!"

Before they had time to do anything the trailer door swung open full force and Sheriff Vanderpool, followed by a deputy and Daddy Joe, packed themselves into the small trailer.

"I told you them young'ens would be here, Sheriff!" Daddy Joe shouted, accusatory like.

The sheriff was sporting the worst shiner that Rita had ever seen and he glared severely at the man who inflicted it. "Well, well what do we have here?" the sheriff asked as he walked menacingly toward them. He put an arm around Rita and Billy and walked them slowly toward the door. "You big city cops think you can do whatever you damn well please when you come to the country. You'all think we're a bunch of stupid hicks out here in the sticks. Well, I got news for you city boy . . ." the sheriff paused as he handed the two over to Daddy Joe, who immediately grasped their arms roughly.

"Listen, Sheriff," Nathan pleaded. "Don't let that man take them. If you have to put them in jail for a night, do it, but don't let him take them."

"The only one who's going to be spending time in jail is you city boy," the sheriff stated smugly. "Nathaniel James Rivers, you are under arrest . . ."

"On what charge?" Nathan protested.

"Assaulting an officer, harboring runaways, to name a couple." He reached for his handcuffs. "You have the right to remain silent. If you give up that . . ."

"I can't believe it! Then it dawned on him, "Rita, you are 18 you don't have to go." He reached out toward her and his eyes searched her face. His look of longing seemed to mesmerize her.

"And let Billy go alone?" She winced at the thought.

Joe laughed at Nathan with a look of pure satisfaction on his smug face, as the sheriff continued to read him his rights.

Daddy Joe roughly escorted Rita and Billy out of the trailer and down the two-track road to an awaiting squad car. He didn't even care that they were shoeless and without their coats. The farther they were from the trailer the meaner he became until eventually he was pulling Billy by the ear and Rita by the hair of her scalp.

"Where's your ma?" he interrogated as they started to drive away.

"I don't know!" Rita cried.

"Don't you go lying to me, girl. If you know what's good for you, you'll start telling me everything you know."

"I'm telling you all I know, Daddy Joe," she lied. "She's probably off somewhere getting drunk. I don't know where she is . . . and I really don't care. For all I know she's went and killed herself? Have you checked the chicken coop at the house lately?"

"Don't you get smart with me, Missy!" Daddy Joe growled as he pulled hard on her hair.

Rita did not know the man who was driving the squad car. She was embarrassed by the fact that he saw and heard everything, but took comfort in guessing by his expression that he seemed sympathetic as he watched what was happening from his rearview mirror.

"Well, it don't matter anyhow 'cause when she finds out that you and the boy are with me she'll be high-tailing it back home quicker than a scared dog puts his tail between his legs."

She had thought that Daddy Joe knew Mama better than that. There was no way Mama would come back home now, unless of course she was on the arm of Papa. She wasn't about to fill him in. At this point it seemed she and Billy were valuable pawns in a dangerous game of deception, and they were safe at least until Mama returned home.

During the rest of the ride home Daddy Joe was silent, lost somewhere in his small mind. Rita watched him from where she sat in the back seat of the car. She wondered why he was so hell-bent on tormenting them. Maybe his hatred for her began because he could sense that she thought he was evil? Or maybe he just didn't like her because she reminded him of Papa; the man who at one time was his best friend, but now it seemed he despised with a vengeance. Daddy Joe had always been nice to Betty and Sally, and never once to her knowledge did he ever hurt his daughter Linda. The only time he was mean to Billy it seemed was when Billy was with her. But she and Rick were treated badly from the beginning. They were the ones who received the brunt of Daddy Joe's rage. Now she could not help wondering why. She scrutinized him more thoroughly at that moment than she had ever dared to.

She had always disliked him, even when Papa was alive. There was just something about him that never settled with her. But looking at him now at close range she begrudgingly admitted that if she had never known him for the demon he was, and had never been subjected to his slobbish ways, she would have thought him attractive in his own right. He had thick blonde hair with red highlights that covered his perfectly shaped head. He chose to wear sideburns, and a light, well-trimmed beard covered his strong chin. His teeth were perfectly straight and miraculously white.

The one feature that took away from his good looks were his dark brown, almost black, beady little eyes. Their physical appearance, however, is not what made them unattractive, it was what you saw when you looked into them, and what she saw most of the time was hate, pure and simple.

She glanced at Billy and noticed he was very pale. His eyes, wide with fear, were fixed straight ahead. She wished with all her heart she could have thrown Daddy Joe out the door of the car, and once again she and Billy could be as carefree as they were, only moments before they were discovered at the trailer. She was fantasizing about throwing Daddy Joe out the door, when she vaguely heard him say to the driver, "Can't you step on it?" Then he whispered harshly to them, "You just wait until I get you in the house!"

Billy looked so scared.

"What the hell is wrong with you boy?" Daddy Joe hissed as he raised his hand to slap Billy. The blow was quick and hard, and it left Billy a bit dazed. It was the first time Rita ever witnessed Daddy Joe hit him, and it hurt her more than any physical pain he had ever inflicted on her. Relishing the look of rage his cruelty provoked from Rita, he raised his hand to hit Billy again, but then thought better of it, probably because the driver seemed to be watching their every move.

****

Nathan cursed under his breath and glared with hatred as he watched Joe grab Rita and Billy. *I'm going to kill that bastard.* When Joe was out of the trailer, Nathan whirled around and faced Sheriff Vanderpool, "Why did you bring him here?"

"Now you hold on right there. I did not bring him here, he brought me here. What was I supposed to do? He came to my house bitchin' that he followed you'all out here and saw that you were keeping his kids. Now you tell me, what was I supposed to do?"

"I guess you did what you had to. Now let me go after them. Be forewarned—if that man harms either one of them, I will take care of the matter as I see fit." The coldness in his eyes did not go unnoticed.

"Do what you have to," the Sheriff granted.

CHAPTER 8

It was snowing when they finally pulled into the drive at Daddy Joe's hundred-year-old farmhouse. Rita hated to be back, her entire being rebelled against it, yet here they were walking the familiar trail that led to the back door of the house. She held Billy's hand tightly. They spoke no words, they both knew better, because nothing had changed between them and Daddy Joe. He would still by his actions just as soon shoot them than look at them. So they walked as though at gunpoint, and it didn't take long for them to get into the routine again. He opened the door and pushed them inside and instantly began ranting and raving as he went to the kitchen to get a beer. They stood frozen in the hall, neither one of them really knowing what to do. Rita was bewildered by how quickly things could change from one moment to the next. After a momentary lapse, however, she began planning their escape. She squeezed Billy's hand just a little bit tighter.

"Why do you have to be so terribly mean?" Billy hurled the question to Daddy Joe. "We've never done nothin' to you."

"Shut up and get your asses in here and plant them on this couch!" Daddy Joe ordered from the living room.

For the first time in her life Rita felt totally unsure of herself. Her, headstrong Rita, having been equipped with what she thought to be an iron will, could feel herself bending slowly but surely. At this juncture it was obvious her spirit could be broken. It was at this time she felt a tiny bit of compassion for Mama. For a moment, she was able to look past the hurt, and for once she saw things remotely through her mother's eyes. Looking at Billy she realized how it might be possible to lose yourself in your love for someone else. Given the knowledge that at that moment she would have done almost anything to rid the fear in Billy's eyes, and would have rather died than to witness any harm being done to him.

Then the blade caught her eye. The glare of the overhead kitchen light made the butcher knife blade gleam brilliantly against the dullness of the corroded oak counter, almost as if it were calling to her. She swiped it without hesitation and tucked it down under her bra in the valley of her breast, cutting herself slightly as she did so.

"No!" Billy whispered viciously.

"I said, get your asses in here, pronto!" Daddy Joe growled as he stormed his way from the living room into the kitchen. He flew past Rita and grabbed Billy roughly by the neck and threw him toward the stairs. "You best get upstairs, boy. That is unless you want some of what I plan on giving little Missy here."

"Daddy Joe, would you like me to rub your back?" Rita asked hesitantly. "Billy, you go on upstairs. Get now," she instructed, while prompting him toward the stairs.

"Well, well, what are you up to, Missy?" he asked in a tone of voice that told her he wasn't going to trust her for a minute. He walked over to his old musty chair and sat down, took a long drink of his beer and ordered her to come toward him. She walked over to him as he took off his shirt, exposing his muscular back and shoulders. She experienced a sudden feeling of shame at how far she had allowed herself to sink. She went behind the chair, reached out and splayed her hands across his shoulders and recoiled as it dawned on her she had never actually touched the vile man before.

"What's wrong, Missy? You ain't never touched a real man before. Lean that sweet little body of yours right up against me sugar. There you go, baby. That's it. That's how Betty used to do it before she went and got stupid on me. Oh, but she was good. But I bet she ain't nothing next to you honey, you feel so good."

Dear Lord, please don't let him feel the knife, he'll kill me! She prayed. "Where would you like me to start?" she asked cautiously

"Start at my neck and work your way down."

Slowly she placed her hands around his neck. They seemed so small and powerless against his massive frame. How she wished they were big and strong like Nathan's so she could strangle the very breath out of the loathsome man.

"Now my shoulders, do my shoulders now. Don't be afraid to dig your fingers in. You ain't about to hurt me, girl."

He was so right. She couldn't hurt him. The deeper and harder she dug her fingers into him, the more he seemed to enjoy it.

"Ah, baby, that feels good. So damn good. You know, Missy, I always knew you'd come around. I just knew it. Yes sir. You do right by me and I'll do right by you. And the boy, too. Know what I mean? Come around here, honey." Daddy Joe ordered. He began to unzip his pants as she came around to face him. "Turn around baby." When she turned around he grabbed her roughly and bit her hard on her rear. She was so scared that she peed. This infuriated, then disgusted him. It saved her from further molestation, but it did not prevent him from venting his frustration in the way of beating her. She kept her arms across her chest so he wouldn't hit the knife. When his anger was spent, she laid there at his feet, battered and broken. She was repulsed by the thoughts of what could have happened had things gone a little differently. She didn't know how long she lay there at his feet, too petrified to move, until she heard him snoring. He shifted positions in his recliner and stopped snoring for a half-second, but once he was comfortable again, he seemed to be in a deeper sleep. She crawled slowly away from him. She thought fleetingly about the knife and was thankful Daddy Joe hadn't noticed it. She took it carefully from where it was hidden and dropped it to the floor. It was stupid of her to have picked it up in the first place. She would never have used it. As she reached the stairs she met Billy. She noticed right away that the fear was gone from his eyes, which, in turn, made her feel less guilt about what she had stooped to do.

"I prayed Rita, and I'm not afraid anymore. `Member . . . fear is the devil's friend, not mine!" he whispered. "I prayed for Daddy Joe to leave you be, so you wouldn't do anything stupid with the knife. I prayed for God to give us strength. We gotta be strong, Rita.

Sometimes his faith amazed her. She wanted to cry out from the anguish she felt at the thought of the many children in this world who have been abused, especially kids like Betty who have had to face the abuse alone. She had, and had always had, Billy, her light at the end of a dark and tortuous tunnel. With him, he brings his prayers. That is what has given her the strength to endure and the will to live these years with Daddy Joe.

"Oh, Billy, what are we going to do?" she breathed hopelessly, as she took in their surroundings. She thought that she saw a face through the picture window. Was her mind playing tricks on her?

Daddy Joe stirred, "Hey, Missy, Take them pissed on pants off, and get your pretty little body back over here!"

Her mind was numb as she cautiously took off her pants and walked aversively toward Joe. He was gaping at her with lust-filled eyes.

"Don't you want to sleep?" she practically begged. "I thought you might like to sleep."

"That's what you get for thinking. Women don't have good heads for thinking." He smiled an evil smile. "This is what women are good for." He grabbed her then, and pulled her toward him. He crushed her wrist with one hand, as he struggled with the other to take off her shirt. "I wasn't sleeping, girl. I was just playing with you, kind of like a cat plays with a mouse, before he eats it. You started this little game of cat and mouse. Now I'm gonna finish it!" He kissed her so hard that their teeth gnashed together. His breath was vulgar, so strong she nearly gagged. He ripped her shirt off as she struggled.

"Leave her alone!" Billy shouted, running toward them with both fists clenched.

Rapidly, Daddy Joe turned and held Rita roughly to his side, at the same time he hauled off and kicked Billy so hard the boy's thin little body flew across the entire living room and landed with a thud against Mama's knickknack cabinet.

Rita watched horrified as Billy lay unmoving. She had a terrible feeling the blow had been deadly, and the thought of losing Billy made something deep inside her snap. The anger and hate she had felt toward Daddy Joe, and had suppressed for the last five years, rushed out of her in that instant. It was somewhat similar to a thoroughbred, at the sound of the bell, lunging out of the starting gate. She turned into a madwoman, escaping the confines of a body that normally wasn't capable of such strength. With all her might she elbowed Daddy Joe at his Adam's apple, and pried herself from his vice-like hold. Once free, with all the strength she could muster, she kicked him where it hurts a man the most. She used such force that she had probably broke a few toes in the process. By his reaction she could tell that he was hurting, but she couldn't stop there, the madwoman part of her wouldn't let her. She kept kicking over and over again in the same spot. He fell to the floor and she continued to kick and jump on him unmercifully. She jumped on his neck, face, chest and groin area. She kicked his side and ribs. All the while screaming a blood-curdling scream. Then she remembered the knife on the floor near the stairs. She ran for it. She was going to end the torture once and for all.

"No, Rita!" she heard Nathan shout from some far off place. Before she knew it he was behind her taking off his coat. "It's okay, honey," he said soothingly as he draped his coat over her bare shoulders. "It's all over. I'll take care of this trash. You go and look after Billy, okay?"

He gently picked her off Daddy Joe, held her until she could stand, and then directed her toward Billy. "I have to look for some rope or something to tie this lunatic up," he explained. "Take Billy out to the car, it's parked down the road a bit. Warm it up. I'll be there momentarily."

"How did you get here so soon?" she mumbled. "I thought you were going to jail?"

"I'll tell you about it when we get out of here."

Billy was trying to sit when she reached him. He had a big gash in his left cheek where one of Mama's knickknacks busted and cut him wide open. Of course she became hysterical once she saw it.

"Are you all right, Billy? Where does it hurt?" Blood was pouring out of the gash and running down his cheek. "Maybe we better not move you? Huh?" She cooed.

"He's got to move to get to the car, Rita!" Nathan snapped. Then on a softer note he added, "He'll be okay. Facial cuts tend to bleed a lot, but trust me, the cut only looks bad. It's probably nothing more than a scratch."

As they walked out to the car Rita asked Billy over and over again if he was okay, until finally he was irritated enough to tell her quite sternly to quit worrying. Then he did something odd. Softly, he began to sing a song that Papa used to sing to them. Rita hadn't heard the melody of it in years. Sweet memories flooded her muddled mind and she began to calm down some. Of course, this was Billy's intention. He was the one who was hurt, yet he worried about calming her.

"Are you sure you're going to be okay, Billy?" She asked one last time.

"Don't worry about me, Rita. You don't look so hot yourself."

He was right. She had a few scrapes and bruises of her own.

They didn't have to wait very long for Nathan. About ten minutes later he hopped in the car, and they were off, to where—God only knew, but Rita didn't care as long as it was far away from Daddy Joe.

After a few moments of silence and a few miles put between them and Daddy Joe, Rita found her voice. "How is it that you got out of going to jail?" It was something that had puzzled her.

"Sheriff Vanderpool is aware of our plight," Nathan said, looking down at her. They were sitting thigh to thigh, and it wasn't until he looked down at her the way that he did that she realized their close proximity and her near nakedness.

"What?" she asked, confused.

"Sheriff Vanderpool is aware of everything that is going on. He knows your mother is in Arkansas. He also knows Joe has been abusing you and your brothers and sisters. I told him about my dad, and that I believed Joe may be connected to his disappearance. But there is no proof. So he must seem to remain on Joe's side. I'm sure you know Joe has many prominent friends, and with a word he'd have the Sheriff's badge, especially if he thought Vanderpool was on to him. As a result the sheriff plays our enemy so Joe will continue to trust him without question."

"Sheriff Vanderpool knows! Everyone knows about everything except me! Why in God's name did you give him a black eye?" Rita wailed.

"He was going to hit you with the butt of his gun."

"So, I've been hit before."

"That doesn't make it right," he said sensitively as he looked down at her with a soft expression on his face.

"I'll be hanged!" Billy hooted. "Sheriff Vanderpool knows . . . I'll be hanged."

His cheerfulness surprised Rita. She looked him over, worried that he might be more hurt than he was letting on. The blood on his cheek was dry. "How's your cheek feeling?" she asked.

He rolled his eyes.

"When we get to Mom's she'll fix you right up, Billy. My sister, Betsy Kay, will spoil you with attention," Nathan warned him.

"Where's your Mustang?" Billy asked.

"Put away for the winter. I parked it in a buddy of mine's barn. I've had this here Falcon for about seven years. In fact, I bought it around the time I first met your ma. It's a little rusty but it runs."

"Tell me about your family," Rita asked. "At least the folks Billy and I are going to meet."

"Yeah!" Billy chimed.

"All right," he thought for a moment then started, "I'm the

oldest at twenty-five, then there's Mary Margaret, she's second in command and follows close behind at twenty-four. She's a schoolteacher in Indiana. Landed a job right out of college. She teaches kindergarten, and is damn good at it. She's the sweetest person, but don't cross her, she can be mean as hell."

It started to sleet then, prompting Nathan to turn his wipers on. Then he continued. "We used to be close, Mary Margaret and I." He seemed to be thinking of another place and time. A sweet smile touched his lips as he remarked, "I miss her."

"When was the last time you saw her?" Billy asked.

"Well, I've been so preoccupied with Dad's disappearance that I only found time to see her twice while she was visiting home from college. I haven't had the chance to go down and see her since she took up residence in Kokomo, but I plan to as soon as I find out what happened to Dad. We talk to each other regularly on the phone, but it's just not the same as having her here. She's one of the few people I know who really listens. It's one of the things I like the most about her. But I hate talking on the damn telephone. I'd rather talk person to person, if you know what I mean."

"Is she married?" Rita wondered aloud.

"Nope, she hasn't found Mr. Right yet. She's been in a few relationships, but nothing serious. Since she was a kid she had always talked about securing a career first before a relationship. She's really into women's lib, and always said she was never going to depend on any man. It's always been a high priority to be capable of taking care of herself. Got to hand it to her, she stuck to her guns and pulled it off. She probably pushed away a few respectable men in the process."

"Where does your mom live?" Billy asked.

"Pine Grove. She's lived in the same house all her life. If you ask me, it's just too damn small to hold eight kids. But somehow we managed to survive all right. Speaking of surviving, that brings me to my brother Pete. He's over in Nam doing exactly that—surviving."

Nathan stopped talking long enough to light a cigarette, then went on. "Pete's not his real name, though. Wallace is. He hates his name. If you happen to meet him someday, do not call him Wallace. He's a good kid, though. The best damn mechanic I've ever known in my life. He's rebuilt the engine twice on this car. He loves tinkering with cars, always has. I'm going to give him my Mustang when he gets back, if he gets back.

"Was he drafted?" Rita asked.

"Nope. Volunteered. The patriotic sort. Thinks he's going to save the world from communism, single-handed. But he writes home every once in awhile, and you can tell he's scared. Not that he's a coward or anything, but he doesn't think he's going to make it back. Too much shit going on over there, he says. He told Mom to tell me I can have his Harley if he gets killed. I don't want his damn Harley. I just want him back in one piece. Safe and sound." He shook his head. "Man, it must be hell over there. You know it?"

Rita thought about that for a moment. Compared to Nam, her problems were zilch. Everyday spelled devastation over there. The Americans were fighting a losing battle, she read in a newspaper article awhile ago. Scores of American soldiers had already been killed. It was a sad thing, the Vietnam War. She just hoped it would end by the time Billy reached the draft age. She looked over at her precious little brother, and tousled his hair. "You okay?" she asked him.

"I'm not a baby, Rita. I've told you a hundred times already that I'm all right." It was obvious at this point that Billy was thoroughly irritated with her concern for him. "Hey, Nathan, how come you're not over there?"

"Nam?" Nathan asked.

"Yeah, Vietnam, how come you're not over there?

"Well, I was never drafted. Just sort of slipped through the cracks, I guess. There is still a good possibility that I'll serve some time over there. I'll do what I have to, but I am glad I have escaped being sent so far. I've been pretty preoccupied searching for Dad, you know. I took a personal leave of absence from work three weeks ago, just so I could put all my energy into helping your mom. I think if she finds your dad, he will somehow have some information about my dad. I need to find out what happened, and until I do, I'm useless really. I have to bring this damn thing to a conclusion, one way or another, or I'm going to go crazy. Enough about me—I thought I was supposed to be filling you in about my family. You do want to know about the rest of my family, don't you?"

"Very much so," Rita encouraged. Billy mumbled his agreement.

"Well, okay then. The twins, Dusty Lynn and Rusty Lee, they put up a pole barn somewhere close to Detroit. I think it is Brownstown. They put up a pole barn in Brownstown and painted a sign: 'Skate While You Wait'. And they're making a killing down there. Kids by the dozen go in there and skate their little hearts out while their parents go shopping at the plaza down the street. At first there were problems with getting insurance, but we all chipped in together to get them started. Mom, Mary Margaret and I, that is. The insurance fees for a roller-skating rink are tremendous. Things were pretty shaky at first, but you couldn't tell it now. It's a pretty nice outfit. I'll have to take you guys down there sometime. Would you like that?"

Billy's eyes grew wide and he started shaking his head yes. "That would be cool."

"I haven't skated in years. I doubt if I could anymore," Rita said skeptically.

"I'll help you," Nathan said softly in her ear, warming her to the very tips of her half-frozen toes.

"Nathan, would you mind turning up the heat? My feet are freezing," Rita implored. She would not have doubted it if her toes were touched with frostbite. All the talk about roller-skating reminded her that she had probably broken a few toes during her battle with Daddy Joe. At this point she couldn't be sure because she had no feeling below her ankles.

"No sense in turning it up now. We're here."

Nathan's headlights showed brightly against a small cottage.

Even before he cut the engine the porch light was turned on to welcome them. When Rita looked up next she saw four or five people filing out the door of the cottage and heading toward the Falcon.

"Hello, Nathaniel," said a beautiful woman who Rita guessed was his mom.

"Nate!" called a young girl.

"Hi, Betsy!" Nathan hollered to her, to be heard above all the commotion. "Everyone, this is Rita," he said as he lifted her out of the Falcon. "And this youngster, this here is Billy," he said, pointing to Billy.

They were greeted enthusiastically by everyone. The genuine kindness that poured out from them took Billy and Rita both by surprise.

"Come in, come in," a young girl offered at the door. The rest of the crowd was still trying to talk all at once. It was all Rita could do to try to listen to each one, individually, at the same time. She was thankful for the length of Nathan's coat. Maybe no one would notice that beneath it she was in nothing more than her underwear and socks.

The room the door led to was dimly lit. It looked to be the living room with two recliners and a sofa crowded around a television. What caught her eye was the bubbling fish tank in the back corner of the room. It was beautiful and filled with lots of different kinds of fish. It seemed so peaceful.

"Hi, Mom," Nathan said as he hugged the woman Rita had guessed to be his mother.

"Nathan, help this poor girl get those sopping wet socks off. I'll draw her a hot bath. Betsy Kay, fetch her a nightgown, a nice warm pair of wool socks and grab my slippers from the bedroom, would you please, dear?" The girl went hastily to do her mother's bidding.

"My dear boy, come with me to the bath. Let's see what we might find to clean that cut on your face," Nathan's mom offered, sweet and motherly like. "Is Billy your birth name?" she asked.

"No, ma'am."

"What's your name?"

"It's William, but I like to be called Billy," he said.

"Well then, Billy it is. Come with me, Billy."

"Yes, ma'am." Billy followed her out of the room

Doing what his mother had asked, Nathan kneeled down and helped Rita pull off her socks. Several toes on her right foot were swollen and severely bruised, maybe broken.

Nathan swore under his breath, then he looked up into her eyes. "I promise you that man will never lay another hand on you or Billy."

Betsy entered the room with a warm towel, a pair of wool socks and what looked to be slippers. Nathan grabbed the towel and cautiously dried Rita's battered right foot, then not so gently he dried her other one. When he finished he fitted her with the socks and slippers.

It was an act so sweetly tender, this wonderful man tending to her feet ever so cautiously. There were no words to convey her thanks to him for his kindness, but she felt she must show him her appreciation somehow, so she bent down and pressed a gentle kiss on his forehead.

At that, he gave her a lovable bear hug, lifting her high in the air as he did so. "You're a sweetheart," he whispered.

She held on to him tightly, not wanting to let him go. "Please hold me, Nathan. I feel so safe with you." She began to cry in front of the few people who were in the room with them. She tried to hide her face in the crook of his neck.

"Betsy Kay, where had Mom planned on keeping them for the night?"

"She told me she would give them her room for the night. Her and Edward would gladly sleep on the pullout. Would you like to take your bath now?" the young girl kindly offered Rita.

"In a little while," Nathan answered. "Thank you, Betsy. I'll be in Mom's room with her," he said over his shoulder.

Nathan carried Rita from the living room into an adjoining

room and closed the door behind him. He laid her on the bed, then sat close beside her. She reached out for him, pulling at him, wanting him to lie next to her. He understood, and did. They laid quietly in the dark cuddled close together.

"How can a tough girl like you feel so damn soft?"

"I don't know," Rita murmured softly. "How can a strong man like you be so gentle?"

"I'm not normally, you bring it out in me. You make it easy to be kind. All you have to do is look at me with your pretty brown eyes and I'm a goner." He held her tighter. "When I first laid eyes on you I knew who you were. I knew you were that defiant little Rita your mother spoke about."

"Mama talked about me?" she asked, unable to believe her ears.

"She did. She told me about all you guys, but the stories she told about you intrigued me the most."

"Like what?" Rita asked. She couldn't imagine Mama saying anything about her.

"Well, she told me about how when you were little you never listened to anyone of authority."

"Especially Mama!" Rita said shortly. "That wasn't very nice of her to tell you that," she complained.

"Why, sure it was. She also told me she knew from the time you were a baby that you had a spirit and determination that just wouldn't quit, something she desperately lacked and how she admired it in you."

"Did she really?" Rita was astonished. "My Mama said that about me? I don't believe you!"

"She did, and she was right, you're a spirited little filly. Her stories about you caused me to conjure up all kinds of images of a girl who I just knew I would like, and I do like you, very much."

"I don't know how you could like me?" she whispered so softly he could barely hear her. "I'm so screwed up."

He hugged her fiercely. "Shhh . . .you break my heart when

you talk that way." He kissed her face and felt her tears, and gently wiped them away with his thumb. "You captivate me without even trying, you know that don't you? Hell, I'd really lose it if you put some effort into it!" he teased. "Right now you're just tired. Damn girl, why don't you give yourself some credit. You've spent these last few years of your life trying to take care of everyone—your mother, Billy, the girls, it's about time someone took care of you. For starters, let's get you that bath!"

Although it was far too short for her taste, the bath was heavenly. Rita hurried it because she did not want to occupy the only bathroom in the cottage for too long. After she got out and dried off, she wrapped a towel around herself and looked about for some clothes to wear, but there were none to be found. There was a soft knock at the door.

She opened it slowly and peeked out. "I have no clothes," she whispered to Nathan.

"Come on silly," he laughed at her shyness, "nobody's going to look." He teased as he pulled her out the door.

They dashed through the living room quite pitifully, Nathan practically dragging her hobbling form behind him. Brilliance struck and he decided to carry her. His laugh, hearty and sweet, made her feel so exhilarated and free she could not help but laugh with him. He made her forget her troubles. When she was with him she was not scared, tired or weak. She was not hungry, lonely or confused. It seemed to her that her soul was on the mend, and Nathan was the magic medicine that was going to save her.

In his mother's room they fell across the bed together. Nathan kicked the door shut behind him as he laughingly inquired, "Did I hurt your wounded toes?"

"You're crazy," was all she could manage.

"Crazy for you, that's for damn sure," he confessed. Then he kissed her soundly.

Someone was at the door.

"Come in," he said, quite irritated by the interruption. "Would you turn on the light?"

"I don't know where the light switch is!" Billy expressed with much animation.

"Oh, sorry Billy, I thought you were Betsy. Don't worry about it, I'll get the light," he said apologetically as he rose from the bed and flicked the light on.

"Here's some pajamas, Rita. That girl out there told me to give these to you," Billy said as he handed them to his sister. "Mrs. Rivers told me I'd be sleeping in here."

"Yeah. She did a real fine job cleaning you up, I see."

"Yeah, she's a lot like Mama," his voice cracked. "Well, I'm tired . . ." he yawned. It was obvious to Rita by his actions that he wanted desperately to cry—but not in front of Nathan.

"Yes, I'm tired too! I think that since your mom is giving us her room for the night, we should take advantage of it and try to get a good night's sleep." She reached out for Nathan's hand and grasped it. Its heaviness amazed her. "Thank you so much for everything."

"My pleasure."

She raised her eyes to his face and caught sight of the movement in the reflection of the full-length mirror just behind him. She looked pitiful—like a drowned rat.

Nathan did not miss the anguished expression that filtered across her face and turned to destroy whatever caused such a reaction. He was a bit taken back when all he saw was a mirror. It was her own reflection that caused her discomfort. *God . . .she was beautiful to him.* How could she think otherwise?

"You know," he started. "In all my life I've never held a treasure . . . then you come along. Tell me angel," he squeezed her tiny hand." How am I supposed to let you go?"

She wanted to cry at the beauty of his sweetness.

He stayed there silently, unwilling to leave her.

"I got it!" he announced breathlessly. He took both of his hands and placed them at the top of her head. Slowly, and ever so softly, he lowered them across her brow and down along her face to cup her jaw. His intense gaze soaked in every detail of her lovely face as his eyes followed the trail his hands had taken. He went on to encounter the feel of her neck and shoulders and the length of her arms. He closed his eyes as his hands reached her hips, and the pleasure he experienced as he pulled her to him was almost his undoing. He could feel her soft breast and pounding heart against his chest as he bent his head to kiss her.

Rita was on fire and feared spontaneous combustion. She could feel Nathan's response against her, and the passion it roused in her seemed at a dangerous level.

Billy tried his best to ignore the scene.

Nathan realized he had to end the kiss before things got out of hand. He stepped away from his little temptress and pretended to be maneuvering something in his hands. His movements were of folding something up as if into a tiny box. When he finished, he displayed his make believe item for her to see, and then put it into his imaginary left breast pocket.

"There," he patted his pretend pocket. "I've captured the image of you and put it in my pocket. Now my treasure will always be with me, right next to my heart. I'll leave you now my lady, to have the sweetest dreams. Good night Billy."

"G'night Nathan," Billy mumbled.

Rita just looked Nathan's way and smiled. She couldn't trust herself to speak. She was too shaky and weak. It was going to take forever to wind down from that little interlude.

Nathan left and Billy cried silently as Rita changed into Betsy's pajamas. She could see his little body quivering under the covers of the beautiful four-poster bed.

She tried to think of something comforting to say to him, to help ease his pain of missing Mama. "I have a feeling Billy."

"What?" He asked through his tears.

"I have this good feeling. Something I've never felt before. Can't you feel it?" She did have a good feeling, a wonderful feeling, and it was all about Nathan. She smiled to herself at the thought.

"No," Billy pouted, "I don't feel anything."

"Try," Rita said soothingly. "Picture Mama and Papa in the

front seat of a big old car, and us kids in the back. Can you do that?"

"Why?" he asked shortly.

"Just do it, Billy!" Rita scolded, softly. "Picture Papa driving slowly down a dirt road on a warm spring day. Can you see it? Can you see Mama laughing and looking at Papa like she was the happiest woman in the world?

Rita crawled into the bed next to Billy. "Dream about that, Billy," she whispered. "'Cause I have a feeling we may see it coming!"

"Really, Rita? Do you think so?" her kid brother asked hopefully.

"Yes, I do. Now you get some sleep. If you're to be any help to us, you're gonna need your rest."

Within five minutes Billy was fast asleep. And a few minutes after that, with warm thoughts of Nathan's kiss still radiating, Rita drifted off too.

****

CHAPTER 9

"Hello, Hello?"

There was no mistaking the sleepy voice of the woman who had answered the telephone. It was Daphne. Helen had found her. Abruptly, Helen set the phone back down on the receiver, and paced back and forth in the confines of the small motel room. Should she call Nathan now? It was three o'clock in the morning, so she decided to wait a little while before she woke the whole countryside looking for him. He dropped her at the Shady Rest Motel yesterday, and before he left he scribbled nine different telephone numbers on a piece of stationary. He gave her instructions to call as soon as she found out anything.

Nervous tension plagued her, and the urge to have a drink became extreme. Her whole body ached. Her parched lips tingled with wanting. It was enough to lead her to the door, but she fought it, and after a moment of agonizing conflict the urge finally passed. This time she fought the urge to have a drink for herself: Not for her kids, not for Richard, not for anyone else but her. With her back against the door she slid down it and began to cry.

****

Rita woke with a start and could hear the murmur of voices outside the bedroom door. She tried to make out what they were saying, but couldn't. Finally, after turning on her side, she could hear the voices more clearly.

"What are you going to do now?" said an unfamiliar man's voice.

"I don't know," said Nathan.

"It's too bad their mother had to run off, leaving such sweet children to fend for themselves. You just say the word, Nathaniel, and I'll look after them," Nathan's mom volunteered.

Rita's heart was pounding. How could Nathan's mother say such a thing about Mama? Even though Rita agreed with her on the matter, she felt that woman had no right to judge anyone, let alone Mama, a woman she didn't even know.

"Mom," Rita heard Nathan whisper. "There is more to it than that. Cut the woman some slack. Don't be so quick to condemn. Had I been in that woman's shoes, I'm not so sure I wouldn't have done the same. It's something you'll never know unless you've been there."

"Oh Nathaniel, you're right. I must stop being so judgmental. But I am only interested in the children and their well being. I care nothing for their mother and her problems. How can I when she so heartlessly left them to fend for themselves?"

Next to Rita, Billy shot up from the bed and was out the door in a second flat. Rita quickly followed behind him.

"Mrs. Rivers," Rita spoke for the both of them in their mother's defense. "Mama is not the best of mothers . . . and Billy and I, deep down in our hearts, we know this. But Ma'am, with all due respect, could you please keep your feelings about her to yourself. It's hard for us to hear our mama being verbally bashed as if she were the lowest scum of the Earth. Although it is hard for you to understand why she did the things she did, for "our sakes" you might try to lighten up on her." Then Rita told Nathan, "We are leaving now. I feel we've worn out our welcome here."

"Oh, dear!" Nathan's mother sighed heavily. "I had no idea you were listening. Had I known, I wouldn't have so drastically bad-mouthed your mother. I'm sorry. Please stay. I would never be able to forgive myself if I was to cause you to leave this house this morning." She got up from the recliner and in the darkness reached for Billy and Rita. "Come here children, sit, and let's talk. We should never have spoken a word about the two of you without your presence."

"Why does everyone blame Mama for looking for Papa?" Billy cried. "Mrs. Rivers, wouldn't you want to find your husband? That is, if you thought he was living?" he asked innocently. "Since Papa died, Mama she ain't never been the same. She turned into someone we didn't know! When Daddy Joe came home and told us Papa wasn't coming back, it was like someone took a knife and stabbed her right in the heart. And then, when Mama and Daddy Joe came home from identifying Papa, my Mama, well ma'am, she didn't talk to me for days. For days and weeks she wouldn't even look at me. 'Cause when Papa went away . . ." Billy was silent for moment, trying his best not to cry. Then he went on, "Well he took with him my Mama. And now that there's a chance Papa might be alive, little by little Mama's comin' back. I thought that someone such as you, Ma'am, would understand what Mama's going through. I mean, I'm only twelve and I understand perfectly! When she married Papa, she loved him more than living. And for a long time you never saw two people more in love with each other than Mama and Papa. Ain't that so, Rita?"

"Yes," Rita defended matter-of-factly.

"And something else, Mrs. Rivers. I'd much rather have Mama leave us kids to take care of ourselves, than to have spent one more second with the likes of Daddy Joe. Believe me, Ma'am, if you was to only know my mama and all that she's been through, you wouldn't talk down to her, I'm sure of it!" Billy explained, meaning every word he spoke with all his loyal little heart. "Even Rita," he continued, "she's the one who has probably went through the most since Papa died, even she understands and forgives Mama. Ain't that so, Rita?"

Billy was definitely pushing it! However, Rita went along with him. "Yes," she stammered for his sake, and then added, "Also,

Mama made Nathan promise to look after us, and so far he's done just that. He has stayed true to his word. And I'm sure Mama knew that would be the case before she left. So actually Mama didn't leave us to fend for ourselves; she left us in Nathan's care."

"Well . . . I'm ashamed. I was wrong and I apologize. I hope someday I meet the woman who has earned such high respect from her children, she must be something to have raised two of the most loyal children I have ever had the pleasure of meeting. Edward, don't you agree?"

"Yes, indeed, Maria. Would someone get the lights? I don't know about anyone else, but all this talk has made me hungry."

"You're always hungry, dear," Nathan's mother said playfully. "I suppose I could fix some eggs and fried potatoes for anyone who's interested. Rita, would you care to help?"

"Okay."

The kitchen, like most of the rooms in the cottage, was quite small.

"Rita," Mrs. Rivers said as she handed the girl a few potatoes. "I have a feeling you are not being completely honest when you speak of your mother. Your feelings about her are not exactly what Billy had in mind, are they?" The older woman paused for a moment, then continued, "If you ever need anyone to talk to about anything, I'm here, and I'm a good listener. Having raised eight kids it goes with the territory."

"Thank you," Rita said as politely as she could, although she knew in her heart she would never be able to talk to anyone about Mama. It hurt too much to think on the subject. She just knew she couldn't bear to voice how she truly felt about it. She looked over at the woman who she had met only a few hours ago. Maria stood graciously over the wastebasket peeling potatoes. As Rita watched her, she wondered why Maria's offer to listen filled her with such a powerful dose of resentment? Maybe it was the fact that in all her life Mama had never once offered to do the same; Mama was always too busy solving her own problems to be troubled with hers. Anyway it would take weeks of talking before it would do any good, and as far as she knew, they would be leaving soon. So she concentrated hard on the task at hand, peeling potatoes, something she had never been very good at.

After breakfast Nathan tried to persuade Rita and Billy to stay with his mom while he went to help their mother. They would have no part of it. They were going with him, period.

"Rita, I wish you would reconsider," Maria pleaded. "You kids have been through so much. It's time you settle down. Nathan has no idea what your mother is up against. He doesn't have a clue as to how long this entire affair might take, and it could be very dangerous. At least here you would be in a stable environment. Please honey, at least think about having Billy stay here."

"First of all, Mrs. Rivers, I want to thank you for the offer. I appreciate it. But I am going with Nathan when he goes. My mind is set. As for Billy . . ."

Billy shot a worried glance in her direction.

"I appreciate your offer to keep him as well . . ." she had a hard time speaking because of the deep emotion she felt. "But I will not leave him. Billy goes with me."

Billy smiled happily toward her as the telephone rang. Nathan's sister picked it up. "Hello. Yes he is. Nathan it's for you." Betsy handed the telephone to him.

"Nathan, here, what's up?"

After a moment Nathan stood up. "Yeah, Okay, got it. I'll be there as soon as I can." When he finished speaking, he slammed the phone hard against the receiver. "If you're coming with me, we gotta go now."

****

CHAPTER 10

Before they left, Billy and Rita were fitted for clothes and shoes. There was an entire closet filled with bags upon bags of clothes, coats and shoes that came from most every member of Nathan's family. They were belongings that were supposed to go to Goodwill, only no one ever got around to taking them. So they were allowed to rummage through the bags. Nathan's brother Eddie helped Billy, while his brother John helped Rita. They offered them whatever they needed. A half-hour later the threesome left with two bags filled with what Mrs. Rivers called necessities and warm blessings from the family still ringing in their ears.

As they drove away, Nathan told them it was their mother he had spoken to on the telephone. She had called from The Shady Rest Motel, near Eureka Springs, Arkansas. She had informed him she had located Daphne Rodgers.

"Is this where we will find Papa, I mean, is Papa with her . . . Daphne?" Rita asked nervously. The thought she could soon be seeing Papa again filled her with joy and excitement.

"We think if your dad is alive, then there is a good chance he is with Daphne, yes."

The mood between the three was somewhat electrifying. Each of them was caught up in their own excitement as they traveled down the highway through southern Michigan toward the Ohio border.

When the thought of how many hours it was going to take to drive to Arkansas became too much for Rita to bear she decided to try to sleep a little. Oddly enough, it seemed that as soon as she rested her head on Nathan's shoulder she fell fast asleep.

Hours later she woke, wondering how she managed to be standing next to the Falcon. "Rita, do you have to use the rest room?" she heard Nathan ask as she tried to focus her eyes.

"Come on Rita," Billy complained, "wake up!"

"Where are we?" she inquired sleepily. "Are we there yet?" she yawned.

"No, we are not there yet, silly. We are at a rest stop in Missouri. Do you have to use the rest room?"

"Yes, I do. What time is it?" she asked.

"Five, it's five o'clock. In other words, you've been snoring away for about nine hours," Nathan harassed playfully. "I stopped at a gas station in Indiana at ten o'clock to fill up on gas and you were out of it. I tried to wake you up to ask if you needed anything, but after the second swing you took, I thought better of it."

"That is so weird, I feel like I've only been asleep for a few minutes," she muttered.

"Well let's do our duty, shall we," Nathan directed.

Rita walked in a daze to the women's bathroom, while Nathan and Billy veered off to the men's room.

It was a dark, dumpy looking bathroom. It did not help that there were about three light bulbs that needed changing. Rita looked into four stalls before she found one with a roll of toilet paper. After getting a good look at the place, she almost decided against using it.

Billy and Nathan were waiting outside for her.

"Was it bad?" she inquired about the condition of the men's room.

"Nasty," Nathan confirmed. "I'm sorry I stopped here now."

"Oh, it's okay, I'm used to using an outhouse, this was far more comfortable," she managed.

They walked around the rest area for a while to stretch their legs. Nathan retrieved some sandwiches of thick sliced bologna and a small jar of mustard from the car. They sat down in the grass as they ate and talked. Billy quickly gobbled his sandwich, then went exploring.

"What was your dad like?" Rita ventured to ask. She found herself wondering more and more about the man that Nathan held in such high esteem.

"Well...." Nathan started, after taking a bite of his sandwich. "I hope it's more like what is he like."

"Oh, yeah, I'm sorry."

Nathan enjoyed seeing her blush and initiated it at every chance. Smiling down at her he began, "He's quiet, very observant. People who have felt his stare say it's as if he can see right through them. One thing about Dad, though, he never could stand people who had a lot to say. He is small, but what he lacks in size, he makes up for in character. Rita, I know you and he would get along fine."

She adored how he said that. "Nathan you are so sweet to me. That reminds me, thanks for the jerky."

"You liked that did you?" he murmured. The way his eyes sparkled, and the way he smiled, it made her feel the heat again, right down to the tips of her toes. It must have showed on her upturned face, considering at that very moment he leaned over and kissed her squarely. Kissing was good, she thought. Nathan kissing her was heavenly.

"We better go," he whispered against her cheek. He studied her for a moment with hooded eyes, a dazzling smile on his face. Then he stood up and offered her a hand. "Hey Billy," he called out to Rita's crazy kid brother, who at the moment was James Bond, agent 007. "Let's go!"

"So, when will we get there?" Rita asked excitedly, as soon as they left the rest area.

"I'm not sure . . . about an hour or so. Why?"

"I don't know I just wondered. I am getting kind of nervous. Gosh, Billy, we might see Papa soon!" She proclaimed excitedly. "I mean . . . what do we say to him? What should we do?" The thought of seeing him again made her feel like a little girl.

"I don't know. We just tell him we love him, and how much we missed him, I guess?" Billy offered, simply.

"Wait a minute . . ." Nathan interjected. "I know that it's hard not to think about all that could be, but you guys better stay focused on what is." He shook his head, "Wait, wait, let me put it to you this way. When I was about 12 or 13, I'm not sure, but I do remember that I was old enough to hunt. I loved to go hunting with my dad. He always told me I was a good shot, and it pleased me to no end to hear him say it. That year at Christmas I remember beggin' him and mom to get me a pair of hunting boots. I thought if I had me a new pair I could traipse all around with them on Christmas morning and shoot me a couple of rabbits for rabbit stew. Dad loved rabbit stew with Mom's homemade biscuits, and I was always so damn willing to impress him. I think I wanted that damn pair of boots more than anything. I'll never forget the feeling that I felt when I opened that box Christmas morning. I was so happy when I pulled off the top—there they were all shiny and new with that "new rubber" smell. I damn near cried. All I could see was my old man pattin' me on the back 'you're the best shot around' he'd say, as he'd rub his hands together in anticipation of the stew. I could feel the pleasure of the moment right then; I was beaming. I took them babies out of that box so fast that I failed to notice one very important aspect about that particular pair of boots. You know what it was?" He looked at Billy and Rita, and they shrugged their shoulders in return.

"They were both left feet! I could have died from the let down."

"I would have worn `em anyway!" Billy stated matter-of-factly.

"Yeah, Billy, me too. But the store my folks bought them from wouldn't take them back if I had. All I'm trying to say is try not to place all your hopes on any one thing, because you're liable to wind up with two left feet! And the disappointment you feel over what you didn't get overrides the blessing of what you have. You miss out on so much when you look at things that way. In my case, it was the last Christmas I had shared with Gramps, my Dad's dad. He died of cancer the following November. I don't remember much of what happened that Christmas day, except about the boots. I have been told about it many times since then, by family members' reminiscing. I have heard countless times about how Gramps and Gram were dancing and laughing and having a ball that day. I don't even remember what they gave me for Christmas that year, and that hurts now. All I really remember is the disappointment I felt about the boots." He cleared his throat, "So think about it. You two have each other, and no matter what happens you have that. When we meet up with your mom you don't know what you're going to find. Time has a way of changing people. Plenty of time has passed since you have seen your dad. So in times of doubt, rely on what you know, and you know you have each other, right?"

It amazed Rita that Nathan was so sensitive. She had never met a man like him in her entire life. His story warmed her heart, and compelled her soul to look at what was really important. He was right, there was no sense in worrying over all that could be, when her efforts would be better spent managing what was.

They came upon a sign that read, 'State Route 23, Eureka Springs, 6 miles'. The butterflies began their invasion of Rita's tummy. She grabbed for Billy's hand and squeezed it, as they looked at each other with grand expressions; it was as if they were saying . . . *no matter what, we have each other.*

"Oh yeah," Nathan said appreciatively, "Good tune." He leaned over and turned the radio up.

Wow, Rita thought, *he can sing.* She had never heard the song before, but Nathan knew the words by heart. The beauty of his voice sent her to paradise as he leaned toward her, "With you . . . my brown-eyed girl . . ."

She swam in the pleasure of the moment. Sweet waves of warmth assimilated even to the coldest depths of her. Every part of her felt alive and waited in anticipation for the next sensation that his display of talent would bring. By the time the song ended she was starry-eyed and weak in the knees: This guy was too much.

Ten minutes later they pulled into the parking lot of

Springville's Shady Rest Motel. Nathan went inside to inquire about Mama.

As Rita watched him go, there was a soft knock against the back window of the Falcon.

There was Mama standing outside in the neon-lit parking lot with tears streaming down her face. Before Rita knew it, Billy flew out of the car and into his mother's arms. There was no sign of the man-wanna-be that Rita had come to know the last few days. Instead, her kid brother bawled in his mother's arms like a newborn baby. Rita felt the hot sting of tears and tried desperately to hold them in check. To no avail, they flowed.

It was on that cool November night outside the Shady Rest motel that Rita looked at her mother and saw a woman she did not know. She realized suddenly she had never "really" known her mother, and it was at that very moment she vowed to herself that she would strive to, and do so without resentment. In other words, she would try to forgive her. But never, under any circumstances, would she forgive the black-eyed devil she knew as Daddy Joe.

"William, Rita, I am so sorry." Helen cried as she held Billy. Over his dark head, she watched Rita intently.

"Mama." Rita barely whispered before breaking into sobs and rushing into her mother's arms. They cried together for the longest time. Finally, Nathan informed them of the scene they were making and asked them if they would like to continue their reunion inside. They agreed to without hesitation.

The room was small. A double bed occupied one half of it, and just inside the door a pea green armchair was placed next to a small desk. Nathan put the chair to use as Helen, Rita and Billy sat together on the bed. They talked for hours of past hurts and misunderstandings. Helen told them news of Betty and the girls and inquired about their stay in Nathan's trailer. They talked about good times with Papa, and tears poured again as talk turned toward hopes for the future. Rita found it odd though, that not once during the entire evening did they mention their antagonist, Daddy Joe.

Mama had asked Rita and Billy for their forgiveness many times throughout the night. She also thanked Nathan many times too. She watched like a hawk every time Nathan and Rita conversed, and after awhile she glanced knowingly at her daughter. Helen could still so easily read Rita. It usually annoyed Rita that her mother could read her so easily, but now things were different. Now she found comfort in the knowledge her mother could read her like an open book. It indicated to her that at least her mother had invested some time into trying to understand her: Understanding, once acquired, is a wonderful thing.

Twenty minutes later Nathan decided it would be more appropriate if he spent the remainder of the night out in his car. As soon as he closed the door, Rita felt a complete and utter sadness. Just moments before his powerful presence had filled the drab little motel room with wonder. It bothered her that he felt he had to leave, yet how could she protest. Just before he walked out he had stared brazenly in her direction. It made her want to go to him, but she stayed put as he turned and left. She thought about running after him, begging him to stay and pleading with him never to leave her again. Following those thoughts was the realization of how deeply she had fallen for him. Feelings too powerful to contain threatened to overflow. Fear of being hurt surfaced, making her want to hold her feelings in; yet she knew if she held them in drowning was a possibility. Consequently, after an hour or so of rationalizing she decided to go and join him. Without waking Mama and Billy she got dressed and went outside. She justified her actions by convincing herself she was only doing so in attempt to set up a lifeline. As it was, she was in way over her head.

"What took you so damn long?" Nathan whispered fervidly as he pulled her into the car and kissed her recklessly.

"Ohhh," the soft sigh escaped her lips. How many times she had daydreamed about such encounters with Matthew Odell, a boy at school whom for years she had held a secret crush on. Of course she never gained the courage to even approach Matthew, but thoughts of him made up her greatest dreams. Always after daydreaming about him she would feel ashamed, especially when she believed someone knew what she was daydreaming about. But with Nathan she felt no shame. What was happening with them seemed as natural to her as breathing.

"Girl, I do want you," Nathan's velvety-lined voice whispered. "But not here, not like this." He kissed her softly then guided her head to rest against his shoulder. He began to stroke her hair, as they lay entwined. "Are you worried or afraid of what might happen tomorrow?" he asked.

"The only thing I'm afraid of is facing Daddy Joe again," she answered distastefully, as thoughts of Daddy Joe sent chills down her spine.

"You don't have to worry about him anymore," Nathan's voice was deadly cold when he added, "he will never bother you again."

Rita believed his words. She had to. Her happiness depended on it.

"Don't waste another minute thinking about that bum," he ordered.

She didn't. Instead she thought about the wonderful man next to her. She wrapped her arms around him and closed her eyes. Little fears that the relationship would never last formed in the back of her mind. He would get tired of dealing with her screwed up life and family. But he was the best thing that ever happened to her, and she was going to try everything in her power to make it work. Throughout the night, images of seeing Papa cropped up, and they were nice; but the truth of the matter was, she didn't have much desire to think about anything, or anyone, other than the man holding her.

****

Rita woke with a start as Billy stood outside the Falcon pounding his fists on the hood. "Get up you two! Come on."

"Why you little. . . ." Nathan growled sleepily as he fumbled to open the door and ran after Rita's obnoxious little brother. "You'll have to come back sometime," he mumbled before turning and smiling at Rita. He was a big, sweet, wonderfully handsome, bear of a man, and when his eyes met hers, she felt such a wondrous peace that it nearly caused her to cry. She could not remember ever being so happy. She climbed out of the car and walked toward him.

"Nathan, you make me so happy. I didn't think I could ever be this happy," she admitted before she stood on the tips of her toes and kissed him.

"Rita," Nathan spoke very softly as he looked into her eyes, "you're a dream . . . my little brown-eyed dream."

They walked into the motel room hand in hand. Helen smiled up at them. "I am so happy for both of you. Now," she directed toward Rita, "let's go find your father!"

****

CHAPTER 11

Daphne Rodgers' home was magnificent to say the least. It was a huge two-story stone abode. White pillars gleamed brightly across the porch to contrast the stone face of the building. A guesthouse hid behind the main house nestled in a grove of black walnut trees. It too was made of stone. The stains accumulated from the walnut trees over the years only enhanced the small dwelling's character. A beautifully sculpted wrought iron fence enclosed the grounds of the estate. As they passed it, Nathan took in all the details. He parked the car about a quarter of a mile away. He and Billy got out of the car and walked purposely toward the estate. As they had planned last night, they were to act as if they were stranded, and in need of assistance.

"Mama," Rita whispered nervously, "are you scared?" They were crouched low on the floor of the back seat.

"Not in the least. What can be the worst to happen? I know Papa is alive, and anything beyond that is trivial. Don't you agree?"

"Well, if Papa is alive how do you explain everything? Did he fake his death to be with Daphne?" *Ouch ,why do I do that?* Rita chastised herself. She would have to learn to think before she opened her mouth, "I mean . . . oh, I don't know, it's all so confusing."

After a long and annoying silence Helen finally answered. "I wasn't aware you knew about Daphne. I know your father loved Daphne at one time, long before he met me. But she shunned him when she found out he wasn't made of money. That tore him up. Daphne went on to marry a very rich old man. After Papa and I were married he told me of her. He explained to me that after his run in with her, he just didn't care anymore, about anything. That was part of the reason he was so reckless and wild when we first met.

"Then Daphne's husband passed away. She hounded Papa terribly after that. He told me, of course, but I think he hid some things from me. I'm sure he did have an affair with her. I think he felt he needed to attain some sort of closure in that chapter of his life, and that sleeping with Daphne was the answer. But anything beyond that I just can't explain."

For Rita, it was strange hearing Mama tell her so frankly about Papa possibly having had an affair. It bothered her to think Papa had done such a thing, and yet it seemed to make him more real. There again, like she had done with Mama, Rita had put him up on some sort of pedestal. She really believed her parents could, neither one, do any wrong. In these past seven years since Papa's disappearance, Mama had proven many times over that she was far from being a saint. But in that same amount of time Papa remained up there.

"Gosh, Mama, I can't stand this! Why couldn't I go with Nathan?" Rita cried, her anxiety was beginning to spiral.

"Rita, we explained this to you last night. Daphne would recognize right off that you are Papa's daughter. You're being childish. Just let it be!" Helen scolded.

Rita peeked up and out the back window. She watched Nathan and Billy as their figures got smaller. She couldn't help but feel the need to be with them. She looked at Mama and saw the watchful look on her face. Peeking back at Nathan and Billy she watched them round the corner and vanish into the trees. Her heart raced. What if something happened to them? What if this Rodgers woman saw right through them? Sure Nathan would do all he could to protect Billy, but who was going to protect Nathan? Looking back at Mama, Rita wondered what she would do if she made a dash for it.

In the early morning light Helen's searching eyes held her

daughter's as she snapped, "Rita Lee Klein, don't you even think about getting out of this car!"

****

"Nathan, do ya think Papa's there? Nathan, are ya scared? What are ya gonna say? Do you think she'll let us in? Do ya think she's mean? Do you think . . ."

"Billy, I don't know." Looking down at the boy Nathan wished he could have prevented the kid from having to take part. He ruffled his hair as they mounted the steps. "I really don't know. But we are about to find out."

Smiling down at the boy, Nathan raised his hand in the air and pounded on the door. Shoving his hand back in his pocket, he stood on the porch, his back turned against the wind and Billy sheltered between him and the house, and they waited. After several long minutes Nathan heard footsteps approach the door. Placing his hand on Billy's shoulder he squeezed it tenderly, trying to reassure himself as much as the boy.

The door swung open and an elegant woman with long blonde hair and curvy features stood before them. "May I help you?" Her tone was glacial.

Nathan could feel Billy tense and rubbed his shoulder hoping to calm him a little. He responded to the woman confidently. "My boy and I had some car trouble down the road a bit there," he explained as he pointed vaguely toward the road over his shoulder. "I was wondering if you would mind if we used your phone, so as I can call my wife's brother to come out this way and help me out." He finished a little nervously. The woman was quite intimidating—a classic blonde beauty whose intelligence radiated from behind her icy blue stare.

"Well," for a second she seemed uncertain and appeared nervous about something. After some hesitation she smiled, "Of course, but make it quick!" And then, looking at Billy with a barely disguised show of disdain, she added, "And don't touch anything!"

The look of shame that crossed Billy's face didn't go unnoticed by Nathan, and it was all he could do not to knock the presumptuous woman right off her feet. But instead, he forced himself to smile politely and reply, "Of course not, ma'am. And thanks very much for your kindness." He nearly choked, but managed to spit it out. "This here is my son, Billy, and I'm Nathan."

The woman stepped aside to let them pass through the door. "Pleased to meet you, Nathan. My name is Daphne. Do come in and I'll show you to the library."

Nathan urged Billy ahead of him into the house. He carefully studied his surroundings as his keen gaze wandered from the rich green carpet beneath his feet to the pristine white walls that raised a cathedral ceiling. The pictures that hung on the walls were of people, but none seemed to resemble Daphne. As they entered the library Nathan stopped for a moment and tried to gather his wits. Hanging above the fireplace was a large portrait of a man, a man that Nathan recognized to be none other than Richard Klein.

Quickly Nathan reached out and grabbed Billy's shoulder, spinning him around to face him. Throwing him a warning glance, he raised his eyes to Daphne. She was standing next to the fire, beneath the portrait and she had an intrigued look on her face.

"The phone is there, on the desk, Mr.—," She cleared her throat, "Nathan. I will leave you alone to take care of your business, but please do take care that the boy doesn't damage anything." With a sweeping motion around the room she indicated all the obviously valuable artwork and glassware. Stepping forward and walking from the room she glanced back at Nathan and smiled before closing the doors.

"Nathan that's . . ."

"Ssh." Nathan raised his finger to his lips and smiled to soften the harshness of the sound. "Wait." Nathan turned and walked toward the desk. Picking up the phone he listened intently to the dial tone for a moment before again letting the receiver rest in the cradle. Turning to face Billy, who was seated on the couch with a dejected frown on his face, Nathan crossed the room and sat down next to him. "Billy, you've got to be cool about this, don't let me down boy. Okay?" Billy nodded, understanding fully. "Good. Now we both know who that is in that picture, right?" Nathan motioned to the portrait.

"Hell yeah," Billy nodded again, his blue eyes wide.

"What to do, what to do, what do you think we should do?" Nathan smiled when he saw the look of shock on the boy's face. He felt he had to fill the boy's mind with a mission in order to put the portrait out of his thoughts.

"You're asking ME what to do?" Billy whistled his anxiety at the thought. "You're the cop."

Nathan couldn't help but laugh. "Yeah, kid, but you're here too, and whatever I decide to do is going to affect you just as much as it does me. Now, what do you think?"

Billy still looked incredulous but straightened himself to look the part. He thought for a moment before smiling and answering, "Well, I think we should beat the old broad up, find Papa and take him home."

"Billy," Nathan laughed nervously, "You have got to keep it down kid, someone might hear you. Now do you really think that she would cooperate with us if we did that?"

Billy was quiet for a minute. "No she wouldn't be able to, she'd be out cold."

Nathan smiled, "Yeah kid. If only it was that easy. But you can bet the old broad is not here alone. Wouldn't you agree that by beating her up, we might be putting ourselves, and your mom and sister in danger? We can't do that now, can we?"

Billy shook his head immediately confident of this answer. "NO! We can't let anything happen to Mama or Rita!"

"All right, so we agree on that," Nathan nodded. "When Daphne comes back, we just act natural. We'll tell her we spoke with your uncle and. . . ."

"I think we ought to find Papa and to hell with her!"

"I know you want to end this Billy! But you have to be patient. If we act too fast it could cost us dearly. Now we'll tell her your uncle is on the way and ask if we could wait for him here. Be quiet and don't speak unless Daphne or I speak directly to you. I'll get her talking and see what I can find out. How does that sound to you?"

Billy nodded as the door opened and Daphne entered the room. Smiling at Nathan she inquired. "Well?"

"My brother-in-law is on the way ma'am. Would you mind us waitin' here for him?"

Daphne's eyes took a sweeping inventory of the room and then settled on Billy, apparently deciding he had harmed nothing and was on the whole a fairly harmless child, as far as children go. There was something about the child's eyes, though, that seemed familiar, but Daphne dismissed it, as she nodded to the boy's father. "Yes, of course. I'll come get you when he arrives."

Realizing she was turning to leave the room Nathan bolted to his feet and reached out for her arm. "Wait!"

Daphne turned around with a shocked look on her face. She looked down at his hand on her arm and then icily up at his face.

Regretting his senseless action Nathan blushed and let his hand drop to his side. "I'm sorry ma'am, I just had a couple questions I was wanting to ask you. . . ." He let his voice trail off.

Daphne looked suddenly suspicious. "Questions about what?"

Nathan smiled. "Well, like all these books. Where did you ever get so many books?" He motioned to the book lined walls.

Daphne smiled and laughed quietly, as if she were speaking with a small child. "These books were my father-in-law's. He loved to read and he saved everything. His son, my first husband, was like that as well; these are books that have been collected by his family for generations."

Motioning to the picture above the fireplace Nathan casually asked, "Is that your father-in-law?"

Daphne laughed, this time with genuine amusement. "Oh, goodness, no! That's my husband!"

"Oh." Nathan was left speechless for a moment as he tried to find something to say. "Yes," She nodded. "My husband is outside with the dogs right now. He is not much of a reader he is more a doer. I should have thought he might be able to help you with your car."

Billy moved slyly, closer to the woman. Nathan noticed his vengeful look and quickly grabbed his much smaller hand. He looked down at the boy pleadingly before answering the woman. "No need for that ma'am, my brother-in-law is on the way as we speak. But thanks again for all your kindness!"

"Of course." She smiled primly, and again turned to leave the room. This time Nathan let her go.

Waiting several moments in silence, Billy finally spoke in a somewhat desperate voice, "Nathan! I can't stand her!"

Nathan, with long powerful strides crossed the room, and seated himself at the desk. Rummaging through one of the drawers he produced a piece of clean white paper and an ink pen. He motioned to the single window in the room. "Yeah kid, I don't like her much either, but don't worry, she'll get what's coming to her. Look out that window and tell me what you see!"

Billy did as he was told and pulled the lacy curtain aside. After glancing out, he turned back to Nathan and replied, "Nothing, well, the driveway."

"Good." Nathan nodded, before leaning over the desk to scribble rather hurriedly on the paper.

> Daphne-
>
> Saw my brother-in-law arrive outside the window. You were nowhere around so Billy and I let ourselves out. Thanks for your kindness. We will remember you in our prayers.
>
> -Nathan

Leaving the note on the desk he crossed the room, placed a hand on Billy's shoulder and guided the boy toward the door. Nathan listened for several moments before slowly turning the handle and peeking out of the room. After glancing up and down the hallway without seeing anyone he stepped out into the hall, Billy close behind him. As quietly as they could they passed through the hall to the front door where they cautiously let themselves out. Once they found themselves out in the cool morning air Nathan grabbed Billy's hand again and ran across the yard and into the trees. Along the iron fence they made their way back to the road, and back to the women.

Helen was standing outside the car wringing her hands as worried expression spread over her face. "Is he there?"

"Damn it!" Nathan growled. "She went up there. What does she think she is going to accomplish?"

"I told her not to. Has she ever listened to me?" Helen shook her head in a subdued manner. "What was I to do, tie her up?"

"Why didn't we pass her on the road?" Nathan wondered.

"She went through the woods." Helen laughed nervously, and added, "She feels right at home there."

"Mama!" Billy blurted out. "That old woman, Daphne, she's a crazy! She's got a painting of Papa hangin' over her mantel. She thinks he's her husband!"

"You are right about one thing William, the old bat is crazy." After a pause Helen looked toward Nathan as a pool of tears gathered and threatened to spill. "What do you think Nathan, is he there?"

"He's there all right. The question is, does he want to be?"

****

Rita ran through the trees effortlessly. Within minutes the canvas shoes she wore were soaked from the morning dew. Mama was exasperated with her for leaving, to be sure, but it wouldn't be the first time. Mama was just going to have to understand you can't always wait around for something to happen, sometimes you've got to make it happen.

What was taking them so long? Had Daphne recognized Billy? If Rita had stopped long enough to think about it, she would have realized she was being foolish, that Nathan could handle the situation. However, at this point, a rational creature she was not.

Abruptly, the frightening sound of what was unmistakably the low rumble of a growl penetrated her thoughts. Fear arrested her as she turned to stare into the snarled face of a guard dog of some sort. Her limbs went numb, as it seemed her inability to breathe took its toll and oxygen no longer made its rounds to her extremities. The dog was not alone, and the effect of the sight of it paled in comparison to the emotions that the sight and familiarity of the man evoked. Rita stood in a trance as blood pounded in her ears to the beat of her heart. Scenes of the past flashed by as mere seconds gave time to outline her life. Papa was almost unrecognizable to her. His once proud and erect frame now looked vulnerable. His eyes did not seem as bright as she remembered; in fact looking into them as she was now, scared her. He seemed dangerously calm, and his grin that she had so vividly remembered seemed lost in the folds of skin that wrinkled about his unshaven face.

"Papa?" Rita whispered doubtfully.

After a moment's hesitation Richard whispered gravely, "Rita?"

She ran to him. "Oh Papa." The force of her embrace about knocked him over.

"Oh my God," Richard breathed. "How long has it been?" He pulled away for a moment to look down at his daughter. "Let me look at you." He shook his head in amazement; his little angel was little no more for she had grown into a beautiful woman. A lump pressed hard in his throat when thoughts of missed moments consumed him. He couldn't think about that now, he had to get her out of here. If he had only followed his heart he would have grabbed his sweet daughter and held on to her for dear life, but then they might all be killed. He could feel himself hardening right down his core. One had to be hard when dealing with Daphne.

"Papa why are you here?" Rita started.

"No time for that now." Richard spoke softy as if he were trying not to scare her. His voice trembled. "You've got to go. If Daphne . . . if she sees you Rita, she'll kill you. Go child, go hide in the trees.

"But Papa, I can't leave you." The mere thought of walking away from him now broke her heart in two.

"You must," Richard said sharply.

"But Papa," Rita cried.

"Now! Go!" Richard ordered.

Rita dashed back into the darkness of the trees. Her legs felt as if they weighed hundreds of pounds each. Every step that took her away from her father felt too heavy. Then she remembered Nathan and Billy. Papa's words echoed loudly in her ears, "If she sees you Rita, she'll kill you." What if Daphne had recognized Billy? Would she kill him—had she already? In her fury to get to the car Rita did not hear the footsteps that were fast approaching her. Without warning she felt an awesome blow to her head. Unable to turn to see who had delivered it, the last thing that she remembered thinking was, how did Daddy Joe get here?

****

Rita woke blindfolded with her hands tied tightly behind her back. She winced as she tried weakly to pull her hands out of the knot. An exasperated groan escaped her.

"You all right lass?"

Her head jerked at the sound of the stranger's voice. "Who are you? Where am I?" she questioned the voice in a panic. Her head was pounding, and the confusion she felt caused a pain in her head like a vice pressing against her skull.

There was a long pause.

"Bucky Rivers." the man's voice started slowly, almost as if he were unsure of his competence to speak. "It has been awhile since I have spoke my name to another human being. Forgive me if I sound like an simpleton."

"Oh my gosh, you're here!" Rita cried excitedly, momentarily forgetting her predicament as she felt genuine exultation at the news. "I can't believe it, you're alive."

Now it was Bucky's turn to be confused. He didn't even know

the little waif who seemed so happy about his being alive. It really caught him off guard when the girl started bawling.

Rita was so excited to find Nathan's dad living, and next to her, that everything else that had occurred in the last few days took a backseat. Even her meeting with Papa seemed second page news, probably because she had expected it all along, whereas where Mr. Rivers was concerned, his being alive and next to her was a complete surprise. She was already daydreaming about the pleasure it would bring Nathan once he got wind of it. That thought alone made her cry with joy. But her joy was short-lived. This was the pattern in her life.

Papa brought me here didn't he?" she whispered gravely.

"There is a resemblance, although I'm not quite sure he is, as you say, your papa. The man who brought you has been the reason for my existence since my arrival here. I know him as Richard Klein, does that clarify?"

Rita braced herself for the confirmation. Pieces of the past and present were coming together and creating a picture that she did not like. Papa had been the one to knock her over the head, not Daddy Joe. Bound and blindfolded he left her. This was not the family reunion she had been dreaming of. It all seemed so unreal. She wasn't sure if she could take much more. The ups and downs of emotions were too extreme. One minute she would be standing proud, high on a mountaintop, and in the next instant she'd be swept down in an avalanche that could destroy her with its power. Only it never did. It always left her capable of breathing, at which point her innate human need for survival would take over. She sat there in her darkness wondering why nothing ever seemed to go her way. Now she wished they had never found Papa. She wanted to drift back, safe into her own little dream world where Papa was a great man. "Mr. Rivers, what did you mean when you said he was the reason for your existence?" She was grasping here, searching for justification, it seemed she was always doing that where her parents were concerned.

"It's a long story. Let me just say that Klein saved my life.

Sure, I haven't had much of an existence since then, but at least I haven't been pushing up daisies!"

"Papa saved your life? How?"

"His influence saved me, his power over a very rich, wicked and highly influential woman who wanted me dead for knowing too much. I suspect you know Daphne Rodgers?"

"I know of her. I've never met her. She can't be that influential, can she?" Rita complained. "I mean, who to hell is this woman?"

"No, lass, it's not who she is, it's who she knows. Thugs like Paulie Biggs and Geno LaCasto. They were hustled out of Chicago and placed here for her convenience. Of course I don't expect you to know them; they are chump change in what I call the "Big Money" business. Think Al Capone, and you'll touch on the magnitude of what is really going on here."

"The Mafia? Papa is in with the mob? This is too much!"

"No, no, no, Klein is not mixed up with the mob, Rodgers is. She married into the mess. Her late hubby, Judge Hugh Henrick, was an associate in return for a couple of soldiers to do his bitch-of-a-wife's dirty work. She wanted Klein so bad that she had her thugs take his Alaskan guide on "a one-way trip" and threatened to frame him for the murder if he would not surrender to her demand of marriage. It was a great master plan, every detail worked out beautifully, and then I entered the scene and all hell broke loose." Pure excitement filled his voice as he spoke, illuminating Rita's darkness with unbelievable truths.

Bucky was thumping. The facts of his small history were fascinating to him. Meeting Helen Klein had been the key to making his dream of going "big time" a reality. He was getting tired of the small town stuff he had investigated in the past. He longed for excitement, and he wasn't getting it through his work, or at home. Of course he diligently pursued each and every assignment he accepted with concern and enthusiasm, but it was getting old. At first her case seemed routine, considering she wanted the low-down on her hubby's extra-curricular activities. She had nothing to worry about though, after tailing him for a while Bucky found him to be pretty loyal and boring. It was his friend Joe Welch who was interesting. Every night after a hard day's work Klein would drop Welch off at his favorite watering hole, a little dive just outside Detroit, near Novi, where he would rub more than shoulders with a few of the local women. Klein would always go home to his wife, so Bucky, on more than one occasion, tailed Welch instead. It was on one of those occasions that Daphne Rodgers entered the picture, and sped things up. Warning signals went up the moment he saw her enter the bar. She seemed just a tad too classy for the place as she walked toward Joe with a perfect womanly stride, equipped with a body that made it a heart-stopping visage. Bucky knew her instantly because of the photos Helen Klein had supplied. From his point of view it was obvious Joe found her a little more than attractive—he openly consumed her with his eyes. After witnessing a few meetings between them it was clear to Rivers that Joe Welch had it bad for Daphne Rodgers, and the woman knew it and used it to her advantage. During the first meeting, Bucky was close enough to intercept some dialogue between them . . .

"You have to convince him to go!" Daphne ordered.

"He wants no part of it. What do you see in him anyway? He ain't got shit over me!" Joe grumbled. He could not conceal his jealousy.

The blonde goddess smiled provocatively at him and bit her lower lip. "You know where you stand with me, sweetie, you'll always be number one in that department. Richard is more my soul mate, intellectually. I need him to make a full circle in this life."

Bucky figured that Joe could never comprehend anything other than his physical need and desire, and it was probably for that reason he seemed to cater to the blonde bombshell sitting directly across from him. From where he sat, he watched Daphne reach under the table and clutch the object that controlled Joe's fate. With her eyes never leaving his face, she whispered "Let's get out of here." And they did.

Bucky followed them outside where he noticed Paulie Biggs. Thankfully Biggs was preoccupied with surveying the parking lot, and didn't notice him at the entrance of the bar, so he ducked back inside in a hurry. He felt a rush of excitement. He had stumbled on to something big here—never mind that he didn't have a clue as to what.

"It all started when your mom hired me to . . ."

"I know what she hired you for, skip that," Rita interrupted.

"Well, I checked the situation out and everything was squeaky clean. I was ready to inform your mom just that when Daphne Rodgers came into view. I had never seen her with your dad, but Welch was his friend and business partner, so I thought maybe he was their go between. But it wasn't like that at all. After awhile I learned Rodgers and Welch were in cahoots with Biggs and LaCasto. I got to know Biggs and LaCasto real well after a number of run-ins at the Wayne County Jail where they were always getting arrested for something—theft, drugs, illegal gambling, assault, even murder. They always made bail within hours. Everyone down at the station knew they were low-life runners for some hot shot, but no one knew who. That is, until I followed 'em to Arkansas where I met Della Henrick."

"Della who?" Rita asked, as she struggled against her bonds.

"Just a second, lass . . . let me help you out with that. I should've done this first, but I was so excited to find myself face to face with Klein's kid that I got a bit ahead of myself."

Before Rita could respond Bucky was untying the ropes around her wrists and ankles. She felt the blood rush back into her fingers and toes and sighed with relief. But her relief left her as her hands and feet began to tingle and it felt like she was being stabbed by thousands of tiny needles. She jumped to her feet and danced around a bit in an attempt to cut short her agony. As she pulled off her blindfold she heard him behind her.

"What are you doing, lass? Is that some kind of modern dance you're doing?"

Rita couldn't help but laugh even as tears of discomfort began to well in her eyes. "No-o sir! My hands and feet fell asleep!" She turned around to face him for the first time, and was so shocked she immediately stood stock-still.

"Well, darlin' if your feet are asleep you had best keep moving to get your circulation going."

"I...yes, I know but I, I just didn't expect you to look so much like Nathan.

"I do." He rubbed the beard on his chin, as he added thoughtfully. "Hmm, the boy must have changed a lot?" He clearly remembered his eldest son, and by his recollection they did not look very much alike.

"Oh yes you do," The girl assured, shaking her head to affirm it. "Who's Della Henrick? And if I had to be tied up, why aren't you?"

Bucky chuckled. "You jump subjects like nothing I've ever seen."

"Well?"

"You sure are your dad's kid, all right. It'd be easier to steal a bone from them vicious mutts up on the hill than to shake your dad off something once it's got his curiosity up."

The girl just stared at him silently.

"Well, I suppose I'm going to have to answer you now. Have a seat." Bucky motioned toward the couch as he sat back down in his rocking chair. "When Richard brought you in here a few minutes ago he mumbled something about you being a loaded pistol ready to fire. Now I'm not sure what he meant by that, but I got myself an inkling. The reason I walk around here like a free man is because the last time I made a half-hearted attempt to escape was a couple of months back . . . after your old man took me to the drive-in to see *Cool Hand Luke*. I got inspired. Wanted to be just like Paul Newman, a rebel with rabbit in my blood. It lasted for about five minutes, until I heard big Sarelli crackin' his knuckles in the backseat. I know the rules around here and I abide by them. I've been here about . . . well it seems forever now. And BE-LIEVE me it wasn't always this way. That Daphne, she's a mean, nasty woman.

Downright evil. If she had her way, I'd be a dead man. Your dad, he's different. He does what he has to do, but he doesn't get a lick of pleasure out of it. For the first few years here, I spent my time like you were. Tied up and blindfolded, although your dad did come down here and untie me every now and then. He even let me outside once in awhile. I tried every way I could think of to get out of here, but I'll tell you, this place is a fortress and it can't be done. After awhile I figured I was stuck here. Even if by some chance I found my way to the light outside, it would only have been "doused" by one of Daphne's men."

"Once, while Queen of Sheba was on one of her obsessive shopping sprees in Europe your old man let me come up to the main house and have dinner with him and the boys, and when I used the john I noticed a telephone on the counter. The damn thing worked! I couldn't believe my luck. So, I tried to call your Mom, but I didn't have much time, and I didn't get through to her…"

"It was me, Mr. Rivers! I was the one who answered the phone! It was me!" Rita jumped to her feet again, unable to contain her excitement.

Bucky chuckled quietly to himself. "Well, I'll be…"

Rita looked at the floor. "I'm sorry I couldn't help you." She sat back down and looked at him anxiously.

"Don't be a booby, you were just a pup, what pray tell could you have done?" Bucky smiled and continued with his story. "Anyway, my calling didn't do much good. I can't help but wonder if maybe your dad wanted me to call. He didn't have to leave me alone like that. Daphne would have had a fit if she'd known I was free man inside her realm with them, but things were laid back when she wasn't around. Don't get me wrong, if I jumped out of line I'd be put back into place real quick." He paused, "You know I almost think he wanted a way out of there. I could have called the locals, but I didn't want to get him into a fix, he'd always been good to me."

"So, who's Della Henrick?"

"I'm getting to that. How much do you know about Daphne?"

"Just what you've already told me. And that she supposedly had an affair with Papa."

Bucky nodded. "You recall I told you she was married to an old Judge, Hugh Henrick? Old Hugh died back in '59, the official death certificate says it was natural causes, something about pneumonia—I doubt that. You see it was right after he died, well, that's when Richard came up missing. Of course, that was the plan. Did you know that Daphne inherited a lot of money from the old man? He only had one kid, Paul, from his first marriage. Paul and Daphne were just about the same age, and I think Paul knew that Daphne was just after his old man's money. He was kind of bitter about it but it made no real difference to him. You see . . . he was a lawyer living down in New Orleans and doing real well for himself. That's where Della comes in. She and Paul got married back in '51. Her maiden name was Frazier, that mean anything to you?"

Rita shook her head. "Not a thing."

Bucky smiled. "I figured as much. You young kids don't appreciate those kinds of things yet. Della comes from the Raleigh Fraziers, the same Fraziers that own the Green Leaf Tobacco Co. Anyway, Della comes from money too, so Paul didn't really want nor need his dad's money. It was kind of the principal of the issue that mattered, because he knew, or thought he knew what Daphne was about. Paul never bothered to contest the will; he just set his mind to spreading the word about Daphne. You aren't from the south, so I don't believe you know how it is down here. Gossip spreads faster than a wildfire and it didn't take long before Daphne got wind that the old Judge's son was bad mouthing her every chance he got. Big blunder on his part—got him killed. That's when I met Della, right after Paul's funeral. She put me on the trail of Biggs and LaCasto. They were high tailing it out of Jonesboro again. It was the third trip they'd made since I had been keeping an eye on them so I followed 'em. I figured I was about due to find out just what to hell they were about. I ended up following their sorry asses all the way to Detroit, then back down south to Miami. The bums were running drugs . . . and not just your run of the mill dope either. We're talking heavy stuff, lass. Just about anything. If you could lick it, smoke it, swallow it without droppin' dead, they were dealing in it. So, after Miami they headed for Jonesboro again. I was hot on their trail and followed 'em here. I'm ashamed to say they busted my ass. You must know, lass, how hard it is to look inconspicuous in the middle of nowhere. I was being a little careless too, which certainly didn't help. That big ape Sarelli dragged me into the house by the scruff of my neck. He wasn't at all gentle, damn near broke it. Anyway, he drags me into this formal sitting room where I come face to face with Daphne, Biggs and LaCasto for the first time. Sarelli tells 'em I was snooping around outside and Biggs and LaCasto are chomping at the bit to take me out back and shoot me dead. Daphne had other plans though. Instead, she convinced them to keep me as if I were a stray kitten or something."

Bucky snorted derisively before going on. "She says I might come in handy on the trip to Alaska, in case Joe hadn't followed through with his plan to hire a guide. I didn't have a clue to what the woman was going on about, I was just happy to be breathing. The next morning Biggs and LaCasto tossed me in the backseat of their convertible. Sarelli came with us. I was petrified, and the boys knew it. They thought they had me fairly well convinced there was no escaping them so they never bothered to tie me up. And I tell you, lass, they did! After seeing how excited they were to kill me in the first place I wasn't about to do a thing to cross any of 'em. It was a slow trip. We didn't drive very far on any one day because they had to stop at every casino, bar and whorehouse along they way. I had the privilege of hearing every single, gory detail about every crime them two idiots had ever committed. That's when I got the lowdown on Paul's murder. Paul the Judge's son, the lawyer, remember?"

The girl shook her head enthusiastically.

"Well, on a whim Daphne sent her boys to take him out. It

was an awful death, ruled an accident. They found him dead in the shower of his hotel room. Poisoned by the fumes of ammonia and bleach, mixed. The damage to his esophagus and lungs was enough to kill him, but it was his kidneys failin' that did him in. Even Sarelli cringed when they described that one. He was small time in comparison to Biggs and LaCasto, pretty much a personal bodyguard for Daphne at the time. I believe he was sent along on the trip to prevent the other two from having a little fun with me, if you know what I mean. He didn't deal in the drugs and the murder, although I don't think he'd have hesitated if it came down to it. I wouldn't say I ever became friends with any of those men; but honestly, you ride in a car with them for that long knowing it's either get along with them or be killed and by God it becomes an awful lot easier to get along with them. It took us a little over two weeks to get there. Am I boring you?"

"Are you kidding? This is better than a Cagney movie! It's funny though, Nathan said you weren't much of a talker."

Bucky liked this little tidbit of information, and smiled his appreciation. "He did, did he? He's one hell of a kid, chip off the old block. In my defense, I have to say that I've spent too many hours listening to the maddening tick of a clock; the shit gets old—I've been reformed. How to hell is he anyway?"

Of all of his kids, Nathan and he had shared the best relationship. Bucky knew he hadn't been much of a father to any of his kids; he didn't have a clue on how to be one. He always thought that Maria did a fine job raising them, and figured he was doing his duty just by going to work every day, and every once in awhile teaching the boys a "thing or two" on how to be a man.

"He's . . ." she hesitated. There were many things Rita could spout off about Nathan. But she didn't want to make known to Bucky her feelings about his son, not just yet. "To be honest with you I haven't really known him very long." she admitted. "From what I have seen he spends most of his time searching for you. He is going to be so happy when he sees you. I can't wait!" She ran her fingers through her hair, rubbing her head softly. "I have the worst headache," she said as she massaged her temples. "This is all way too much. You know, I feel like I am stuck in a never-ending dream."

"Well, darlin'," Bucky said, "welcome to my world."

****

Nathan raked his fingers through his thick hair. "If he chose to be there it means he's just as bad, or worse than the rest of the hoodlums. I wish she wouldn't have went off half-cocked, we could have thought this out more thoroughly. As it stands, I say we get the locals involved, she's in danger."

"Papa doesn't wanna be there! What locals are you talkin' about?" Billy yelped, a little on the defensive.

"Local boys—police, come on Billy. All the better if he is being held there against his will, I hope that to be true."

"What if it isn't true?" Helen wondered aloud. "He'll go to prison . . . I don't want to lose him again."

Nathan looked at her coldly, distrustfully he asked, "Are you prepared to jeopardize your daughter's life to prevent that? I'll tell you right now, I will not let you do it. I am going into town to get the locals, now."

"Me too! Come on Mama." Billy pleaded.

"I better stay here in case she comes back, don't you think?" Helen directed to Nathan.

"I'm glad somebody is thinking," Nathan grumbled. "To be honest with you . . .I don't know what I'm doing." He looked up toward Helen and shook his head in disbelief. "That girl gets to me, I'm acting brainless as all get out when it comes to her. It's beginning to irk me." He shakily pulled out a cigarette, lit one and took a long drag. "All right Billy, let's go."

Helen watched them speed away before she headed in the same direction her daughter had taken a half-hour earlier. It was rough terrain. The thick woods seemed impenetrable, and after a few minutes she felt drained. About fifty feet in front of her she heard something crashing through the bushes, She followed the sound to a little clearing where the grass was fine, soft and billowy. When she looked down she saw the clear outline of where a deer had bedded down. She knelt and felt the imprint it had left—it was warm and dry. Five feet away there was a row of boulders. Helen guessed by the appearance of the place that the land had once been farmed, years ago. Young, spindly oaks and poplars fought their way up toward the sun. There were lots of underbrush, and seedlings too. Whoever owned the place must have moved the rocks there, symmetrically, out of the way, so that the land was free to cultivate. It looked like the perfect spot to rest and regroup. She sat on the flattest rock, tucking her knees to her chest as she rested her head on her arms and listened to the sounds of the young forest. After a moment all she could think about was the possibility of finding Richard only to lose him again. In her mind there was no explanation for his being here, except that he wanted to be, and in that case he was a criminal of the worst kind—inflicting much pain on his own family. She began to cry softly, mournfully. The sound was haunting as it combined with the early morning mist to create an eerie sense of mystique about the place. Richard observed the entire episode form a short distance away. It was a powerfully moving scene, his beautiful Helen, always so soft and shy and ready to please. She was there, twenty feet away. The sight of her alone had made him weak, but her cry tore at his very soul. All threads of reasoning vanished. He only knew to comfort her, for she truly was his love, his life, unending.

He went to her, and as he reached for her, she knew it to be him. She was not startled, nor excited, only at peace. They cried together, their bodies swaying in rhythm with each emotion they expressed. Even though they were both weak from past events, which had taken their toll, they held each other mightily. At that moment the bond they created between them could not have been broken by any power under God.

"Richard . . .I knew it," Helen whispered, as she looked at him through her tears.

"You're here, and fine."

"My God, Helen, how many times I have prayed for this . . . dreamed of this . . ." He kissed her deeply. "I don't know how in the hell I managed to go on here . . . without you." He closed his eyes and held her tight. "I don't know what to say? I'm so sorry. I can only imagine what you and the kids have been through."

"Oh Richard, Rita . . .we have to go and find her. She's looking for you."

"She found me."

"What?"

Richard laughed nervously and shook his head. "She's beautiful—she looks just like you." He stared at his Helen intensely, soaking her in. "I couldn't believe it, I still can't. She caught me totally unaware, I had to do something with her before she got us all killed."

"Where is she?" Helen cried. "What did you do to her?"

"I hit her. I had to knock her out!" He raised his hands in the air in abandonment. "I didn't know what else to do. I figured a bump on the head would be better for her than her having her head blown off by Sarelli."

Helen was taken aback by his words.

"You've got to go too!" Richard warned. "You have got to get out of here before . . ." his voice trailed off as he shook his head in grief. "Damn! We're all done for! We can't win this one. I don't see a clear way out of this."

"Oh phooey! I am so tired of this. You want me to turn around and leave here . . .pretend that you're dead? Do you think I could? You better be ready to hit me too! But you're going to have to do while I'm looking you square in the face because I'm not turning my back on you. Not this time, not ever again!" She reached for his hand. "Look at me. I am stronger than you think, and not all together stupid—I have this . . ." She pulled out a .38 special. "I am going to get my daughter, are you going to help me?"

"For Christ sakes Maggie . . .it's not that simple."

"It's okay, it's okay. Don't worry Richard, Nathan went to get some help in town, he should be here any minute."

"Oh that's just great! Who to hell is Nathan? Daphne owns the cops around here; this Nathan will be walking right into her grasp. Who else is with you? You might as well consider them dead!"

"Billy is with him," Helen breathed, her eyes were big a saucers.

"Well hell Maggie, why didn't you just bring the whole damn family? Give me the gun." He grabbed it from her. "Is the damn thing loaded?"

"It's loaded." She quipped. "We can do this Richard. We can do anything when we're together."

Richard smiled nervously her way, but he obviously had his doubts.

****

Direct the Shards

There is a force that I have felt so many times
Anger, not rage
It encourages me when I let it
It leads me to take action
Actions that cannot be undone
Actions that remind me of tracks made by a survivor of an avalanche
Unscathed by the power of the rumble
Steps coming from nowhere leave their mark in the snow
Screaming I'm still here you thought you had me
Emotions keep rollin' out of control
"I Have A Dream…"

Anger is never good?
Depends on the angle
If eloquently portrayed it might even pass as an expression of love
The word "love" is too pretty for me
I'd rather say it plain
Doesn't love produce the worst kind of pain?
In a world where violence outlines the day
Don't confuse anger with hate
Hate produces anguish
Anger can produce change
Change is good

CHAPTER 12

Rita put her head in her hands and looked at Nathan's dad through her fingers. "Where are we anyway?" she asked.

"We're in the guesthouse, behind Daphne's place."

"And there is no way out of here? I find that hard to believe . . ." She got up and went to the window, there were iron bars across it.

"Believe me lass, I have checked every nook and cranny in this place, it's escape proof." He followed her around to each window. "I told you," he affirmed after she checked each one.

"I'm not finished!" she declared, as she walked over to the back door and turned the handle: It was unlocked. "Holy shit!" she yelped as she looked toward Bucky with wide eyes, an outrageous smile of disbelief on her face.

"You have been paying attention to me, huh, lass? You can't walk out that door." He shook his head before he added, "Sarelli is probably right around the corner."

She laughed nervously at his reaction. "I'm going . . ."

"This is not funny," he held up his hands pleadingly, "d-o-n't do it!"

"Why? I'm not going to sit here and wait around to die."

It was a bold statement coming from nothing but a little bit of a girl whose conviction packed quite a punch. Her dark eyes gleamed with determination as she added, "I have spent my life sitting and waiting for other people to take action for me. If I sit on this . . .what's going to happen? I'll get to spend the rest of my life in this shabby little guesthouse with you! No thanks."

Bucky looked hurt. "Well, no need to get personal."

"Aren't you tired of being a prisoner here? Don't you want to see your children? I don't understand you and Papa, aren't you angry?"

"Hell yes I'm angry!"

"Well . . ." she shouted, "direct your anger and fight for your freedom!"

"A lot of good my freedom will do me if I have a bullet lodged in my brain."

Rita raised her eyebrow and said, "Well, then you'll really be free."

He looked at her incredulously and finished, "No, then I'll really be dead."

Bucky closed his eyes and shook his head in an attempt to clear it. Klein was right. His daughter was every bit the spitfire he had claimed she was. The girl's bravery was starting to get on his nerves. He felt like a coward, and it wasn't at all flattering to his ego. He could have killed Klein for getting sloppy and leaving the door unlocked, and himself for having untied her. Now he had to do something. There was no way he was going to let the little waif get 'em killed.

Rita looked out the door.

"What do you plan to do?" he questioned.

"I am just going to make a run for it."

"Come on girl, I know you're not crazy. Daphne's men are going to shoot first, and pick up the bloody pieces to solve the puzzle of who you are later. I appreciate your gumption, but you're not going to get very far if you try to run for it. Now, shut the door! " He commanded with a steely tone.

Rita complied without argument; there was something in his voice that demanded it.

"Now listen to me. I've spent many years watching my P's and Q's around here in an attempt to keep from becoming food for the fishes of the White River. If we're going to get out of here, we have to do it with a plan." He let out a nervous sigh. "But . . . before we go off and get ourselves killed I think I should come to your old man's defense. You said you didn't understand him? Well, before I met him I didn't understand him either. I thought he was a coward, pussy-whipped, you know? But I was wrong, and I realized it once we got to Alaska. The boys took me to an underground cave somewhere near Anchorage. They had been warning me all that morning that I had better make amends with God because I would be facing Him soon. Sarelli didn't follow us down into the cave. He was claustrophobic as hell and couldn't get past the image of the cave crumbling down around him. The boys were a little apprehensive too, but they doped themselves up to where they were higher than Mt. McKinley to get over it. They had a couple of ice picks and it got me picturing the worst kinds of deaths, especially since Sarelli wasn't going along to keep them from having their fun. I figured I was as good as dead anyway, so I wasn't too worried about going down into the cave. When we got down into the slippery blue-black depths, we met up with Joe. He asked the boys about me, and they explained I was a backup body. He was furious, said something about it being bad enough that he had to take part in the murder of one sorry sap on account of Daphne's romantic notions."

"The guide?"

"Yep. He never had a chance, and it looked like it was the end of the line for me too."

"What happened?"

"Well, the next thing you know two men are making their way toward us. The big one, your old man, he says to Joe 'What the hell are they doing here?' Before Joe could answer, Biggs slams the side of his pick across the guide's face. It was a hideous sight and sound. I think that first blow killed him instantly, but Biggs let him have it again anyway right across the side of his head. The guide fell against the cave wall and Biggs hit him one more time across the face. By that time I closed my eyes like a scared kid. But your old man didn't. He jumped between the two—a little too late, but he didn't know it. He beat the piss out of Biggs. It took

Joe and LaCasto to pull him off. When I opened my eyes during the skirmish I looked at the guide, he was obviously dead. The sight made me puke my guts up. I had seen dead people before, but I never witnessed the act of murder, and I can say with passion that I never want to again. That's why I don't want you to go out there, girl." He looked at her pleadingly, then went on, "After Joe and LaCasto used a little muscle to calm your old man, Joe told 'em Daphne's deal: If he went directly to her without causing a stir, no one else would get hurt. Your old man wasn't buying it, and told 'em to tell the dreadful bitch he'd rather die!' But Joe warned him that if he died before returning to Daphne, she would go ahead with her plans to torment and kill several members of his family, starting with his precious wife. I'll never forget how anguished your old man sounded when he agreed to go quietly. LaCasto raised his pick to bump me off, but Klein told 'em, 'no one else gets hurt—that includes him.'"

"LaCasto argued with him, but your old man told 'em, 'If he dies, the deal's off.'"

Bucky swallowed hard. "I owe him you know. Back then I don't know if the circumstances were reversed if I would have done the same for him. But after having known him for awhile, I sure as hell know I would do it now."

"So Papa really didn't have an affair with her. I knew it. I just knew it." Rita began to rub her head again. She was hurting inside and wanted to cry, but couldn't. It was like she was out of tears—dryer then a dead cactus. She looked toward Bucky enviously because at this point he knew her father better than she did. It bothered her that she could be so jealous to worry about such trivial things, and she silently berated herself for it.

"No, I don't believe he did," Bucky agreed, then asked with genuine concern, "Are you all right lass?

"I'm all right. I just wish that Daphne Rodgers had never been born. Ugh, this is going to drive me over the edge . . . What is wrong with me? I'm like a child in my way thinking, still holding strong onto that romantic notion that good always prevails over evil. But then again, it's a thin notion, 'cause in all honesty, I've got enough hate and anger stored inside this body of mine to kill all of 'em with my bare hands! And in that case I would hope that evil prevails."

"I wouldn't necessarily call that evil, they've more than asked for it," Bucky shook his head in disgust. "But it ain't in you to be the killing kind. I reckon you're just like a lot of college-age kids these days, a lover not a fighter."

"I wouldn't say that," Rita countered." No, I'm a fighter . . . I'm just not a killer. I know that with certainty. I've had the opportunity to kill the worst enemy that you could ever imagine and didn't. Thank God for small favors that I didn't, I could really see myself regretting it now."

"Well now," Bucky began with an exaggerated innocence. "I just can't see a sweet and pretty thing like you having any enemies."

Rita glared at him momentarily then exploded with a hearty laughter. "Oh believe me, I've made plenty of enemies in my lifetime," she paused for a moment, "I see where Nathan gets his sense of humor."

Nathan, the mere thought of him aroused her. Where was he? It was the first time since meeting Bucky that Rita allowed herself a moment to really think about him. She winced as it dawned on her that if she would have burst out the door earlier, she might not have ever seen him again. This thought had a profound effect on her. "So do you think we should lock the door?" she stammered. She swallowed hard before continuing, "You've worked hard at staying alive around here and I don't want to be the cause of you being killed. I've got enough to feel guilty about."

"We can't lock it. We'll just have to hope your old man realizes his mistake and gets his ass back here before it matters." Bucky looked past the girl to the door just as Klein and a woman, Mrs. Klein, barged in. "What the hell..." His statement was cut short by the look of urgency in Richard Klein's eyes.

"Buck, I'm gonna need your help buddy." Richard hurriedly

solicited the older man as he made his way inside the guesthouse. His tone seemed confident, but the pale shade of fear coloring his face made him look very afraid.

"I am ready when you are," Bucky said with a devil-may-care attitude. "I've got some plastic utensils in the kitchen, let me go get 'em. We're going to need some means of defense here." Bucky noticed Helen and her look-alike daughter staring at him openmouthed, "Shut your traps ladies . . . if I am going out, you can bet it will be with a laugh. My life has been nothing but a badly drafted comic strip these years I've spent here, by none other than that Queen of Sheba..." He looked toward the main house. "I'd like to write my own ending."

"Papa . . . I am ready to do whatever it takes," Rita vowed. The girl stood near two feet shorter than her father did, but her stance was proud and erect, and she looked more than capable. Pride welled inside Richard—she was his Rita all right.

"Me too," Helen added.

Well, hell, I feel a hundred times better knowing the two of you she-cats are on our side. Okay Klein, where's Sarelli right about now?"

"He's messing with the weilers, Misty and Rex. He's been workin' on that damn kill command."

There was a short lapse of silence as the quartet let the "kill" statement register and each suffered through visions of man-eating Rottweilers attacking on command.

"I thought you said their names were Biggs and La Casto?" Rita tossed sarcastically toward Nathan's dad in an attempt to lighten the heavy grip of fear that assaulted her.

"We got ourselves a real comedienne here." Bucky kidded right along with her, but the smile he afforded the girl was genuine. "I'm feeling right at home with this little lady."

Richard looked toward the pair disapprovingly. " Believe me Rita, if one of those dogs gets their jaw clamped on you it wouldn't be a laughing matter. I know them dogs better than anyone . . . they're vicious creatures!"

Bucky jumped on the declaration as all traces of amusement left his presence and he exclaimed, "The dogs! Hot damn!"

Richard immediately knew what he was about. "Yes! The dogs!"

"You said it yourself my friend that you know them mongrels better than anyone—you trained them on that command. Sic 'em on our buddy Sarelli, I'd say they'll love you for it; he'll be one tasty scrap."

"Yeah, if it works. If it backfires he'll beat me to within an inch of my life. But he'll spare me, I'm sure—Daphne has insured that much. Give me about15 minutes, if I don't make it back by then, go to plan B."

"Plan B? Right-tee-o. Let me fetch them utensils . . ." Bucky chortled as he walked off toward the kitchen to give the newly reunited family a few seconds of privacy to offer goodbye affections before once again being divided.

Helen firmly held Richard's hand. "Let me go now," he pleaded to her, "before the kid arrives unbeknownst to him with reinforcements for Daphne."

"What . . .what about Nathan? Where is Billy? Are they okay?" Rita cried.

"They'll be fine Rita," Helen comforted. Her tranquil voice seemed to calm her anxious daughter. "Nathan is quite capable you know," she continued soothingly as she felt Richard pulling away. She would not lessen her grip—how could she let him go.

"*I'll* be fine," Richard whispered to his wife. "*I'm quite capable you know.*" And with a soft kiss to her forehead he was gone.

****

The falcon squealed to a halt in front of Springville's tiny police outpost. The old brick building looked vacant, not a squad car in sight.

"We might better try locating the nearest doughnut shop, huh Billy?" Nathan kidded his little companion.

"What?" Billy mumbled, giving Nathan a sideways glance. "Doughnuts . . . mmm . . .okay but we better hurry, we got important stuff to do!"

Nathan felt a rush of tenderness at the utter sweetness of the boy. He reached over and tousled his hair. "You're a crazy kid."

"What?" Billy was lost.

"Come on silly."

As they entered the post Billy hid shyly behind Nathan. A freckled, redheaded woman with a bobbed hairdo sat behind a huge oak desk. She was working over a wad of gum pretty good as she queried between chews, "Hey there, what can I get y'all?"

"Sheriff around?" Nathan asked nonchalantly.

"Nope. They'all went to check on some tag swipers over at Bedford Hills Estates. Y'all probably don't know where I am ta'kin 'bout, do ya's . . . Yer not from around here?" She looked the pair over then shook her head, "Nope, I do believe yer strangers to these here parts. Wha'd ya need?" She continued to work viciously on her chewing gum, as she eyed Nathan from head to toe. "I can get him here in a jiffy . . .that is, if he didn't take a ride over to the Rodgers Place." She stopped chewing long enough to stick her finger halfway down her throat. "Makes me sick how they cater to that woman. The sheriff, he don't like it none to be bothered when he's there, I better hurry up and call him. Maybe I'll catch him on the fly."

"No," Nathan shook his head. "No, we won't be needing the sheriff I guess. Maybe you can help us. You guessed it when you said we were new to these parts. We thought maybe you might point us on the trail to get set up with a place somewhere here in town."

The woman glowed with excitement and smiled flirtatiously at Nathan. "You got yerself a little woman at home?"

"Hell no, ma'am," Nathan stated quite brashly.

"He likes my sister," Billy voiced on his sister's behalf. He openly glared at the redheaded woman. "And we better get back there, she might be in all kinds of troub . . ."

"Billy . . ." Nathan interrupted. "You go on out to the car and wait . . . okay?"

Billy looked up at Nathan hurt, then his face transformed to one of distrust. "Yeah, whatever you say."

As Nathan watched the kid walk out the door he speculated at how the youngster could be so sophisticated one moment and totally naïve the next. Then he turned his attention to the redhead. "Don't mind the boy...he doesn't know what he's talking about." He walked pointedly toward her, his eyes boring into hers as he struggled to give the impression of being quite intoxicated by her. "Why don't you find out where your buddy, the sheriff is? Let's get a handle on how long we might have to ourselves here. It's been awhile for me, but not that long, and you've got me revved."

"Revved huh?" The woman breathed, before she took a moment to admire her reflection in the window. "I'm Roberta. What did you say your name was?"

"Call me baby . . .preferably sigh it." Nathan coaxed. There was a devilish gleam in his eyes as he stared at the lewd, red-faced redhead. "How long we got?" he whispered hotly into her face.

"Give me a minute. Okay sugar?" She took out her gum and licked his upper lip quite cat-like.

Nathan listened intently as Roberta radioed the Sheriff. He overheard that the boys were still taking care of business across town, and would be wrapping it up in a half-hour or so. Roberta mumbled something about lunch to the sheriff and he replied he would be taking it at the Rodgers place. When she turned around to flash an all-clear smile at her new paramour her jaw drooped to the floor for he had vanished.

****

"Billy, I know you're mad. Before you stew too long over nothing I want to make one thing clear—I will do my best not to hurt Rita."

Billy looked over at Nathan for a second then turned his gaze away. "Umm huh. You think I'm just a kid . . . too stupid to know about guys like you? You think I haven't seen it? I saw it everyday with Daddy Joe and his friends. I might be dumb about some things, I did think you were different. But now I know you ain't no different than them." There was a fierce look about the boy as he continued, "You stay away from my sister."

Nathan pondered his young friend's words for a moment. "Billy, I don't blame you for being pissed off, but you've got it all wrong." He shook his head dismayed and proceeded, "but, I guess that's one confusion you're going to have to contend with for the rest of your life, thinking everyone you meet is going to be Joe. Well I'm here to tell you that not every one is like that! I'll admit what I did back there was underhanded as hell. But I had to do it . . . and nobody got hurt. Now I don't doubt for one stinking minute you've seen enough shit displayed throughout your young life to fill the Pacific Ocean. But you gotta be fair to me. I ain't like that man, and I really don't appreciate being compared to him. Got that? You gotta get over this "Daddy Joe" hang up. Not all people are bad, and I have only known a few bums as mean as him. If you give me a chance, I'll prove it to you. I'll show you what good people are all about. But at this moment I would like you to trust me a little—I know what I am doing here." With that, Nathan fumbled around to find a cigarette and could not. "Do you get what I'm saying? You're so on top of things sometimes I just assume you're with me. I forget how young you really are," he confessed apologetically.

"You're trying to say that what you did back there . . . with that lady . . . .well you were trying to um . . . bull crap 'er?"

"Yeah kid."

"I kinda thought so. You were actin' weird when she said that old broad's name.

"When Roberta mentioned Daphne, I figured that "*the old broad"* must be in good with the locals, so getting them involved would probably make things worse."

"I'll bet you're right," Billy agreed. He scratched his head as he admitted, "Well, the reason I got sore, well . . . Rita likes you . . . you know that? She wouldn't like the way that lady was actin'—not one bit." Billy shook his head in disgust. "And if I can help it, nobody's gonna treat Rita like Mama's been treated."

"I admire you for your loyalty to your sister, and I have a feeling she's not going to allow that to happen. She's a lot stronger than you know."

"Oh, I know she's strong all right, but she wasn't there . . . I was." Billy smiled proudly, but then his brows furrowed together. "See what I mean?"

"Yes I do."

Billy's face relaxed. "Since I can remember I have only really been able to count on one thing—God. Well, maybe two things, 'cause most of the time I can count on Rita. I don't know if I can trust you. But you don't scare me . . . I'm not afraid you're going to clobber me or something; and you're nice to Rita and Mama, so you're okay."

Nathan experienced a deep emotional stirring over the kid's confession. He cleared his throat and offered, "Hey kid, you're okay in my book too."

"Yeah." Billy smiled, but rolled his eyes. "What we gonna do now?"

"Looks like we'll have to punt."

"Huh?"

"I don't know Billy. What was your dad like? Do you think he would hurt your mom, or Rita, if he saw them?"

"Not in a million years! Papa would never hurt any of us kids or Mama.

Billy was quiet for a minute, deep in thought.

"You remember when you asked Mama about Papa wanting to be with that old lady, what's her name?"

"Daphne," Nathan replied.

"Yeah her. Well you know what I think . . . I don't think he does. I think he hates her. Seems like I remember when I was little he used to sing this one song. The one that goes, 'Hang down your head Tom Dooley. Hang down your head and cry. Hang down your head Tom Dooley. Poor boy you're bound to die.' He sang that song all the time, and whenever he did Mama would get so mad at him, and I could never figure out why. But I think I know now. I think Papa thought about that old broad when he sang that song. And I think he wished he could have stabbed her, just like that Tom Dooley stabbed that lady. I'll bet that's why he liked singing that song so much. And I'll bet ya Mama thought so too, and she was afraid he would one day!"

"Okay . . ."Nathan cleared his throat. *I've got to set this kid straight.* "Hey Billy, that's a good tune, maybe he just liked it?" Nathan offered.

"Nope, he sang it for a reason, I'll bet."

"You don't really think people go around fantasizing about and wanting to kill others do ya, Billy?" Nathan questioned skeptically, not really sure of the kid's mental state, considering all he might have endured at the hands of Joe Welch.

Billy cracked up, "No . . . why do you say that?

"Well you said you thought your Dad wanted to stab Daphne?"

"Yeah, but that doesn't mean I ever thought he would do it for real…I just meant he probably wanted to is all. Geez, Nathan, don't mind what I say, I'm just a kid."

Yep. Nathan thought to himself. *And kids say the damnedest things.*

****

Richard slithered from one vantage point to the next until he reached the courtyard where Sarelli seemed to be very involved with the dogs. The big goon continued to work with them unwittingly, and never had a clue to Richard's presence. Misty and Rex were another matter, as was obvious to Richard when their heads turned in unison toward him. He knew he had to act quickly, before the buffoon noticed the object of their interest. He took out his wallet and tossed it across the courtyard. The sound startled Sarelli, and propelled him into action. As he moved stealthily toward the sound with his weapon drawn, the dogs relaxed a little, assuming they were released from his command. Like clockwork, Richard crept silently toward them, whispering for them to heel. Once he felt sure the pair were under his control, he hollered toward the big guard, "Hey buddy . . ."

Sarelli twirled around with gun aimed and ready to shoot.

Richard laughed nervously before he questioned, "What's going on?"

"Ahh," the big guy smiled clumsily. "I wuz checkin' on somethin'" he muttered as he made his way toward the threesome.

Richard fleetingly experienced second thoughts as he sized up the giant. The dogs would have to attack at precisely the exact moment. On the best terms the gun would have to be put away, or at least pointed toward the ground. There was no doubt the dogs were vicious, and they would maim Sarelli at the very least, so without another thought Richard motioned for the dogs to be on their guard—instantaneously they took their stance.

"Damn you're good with them mutts . . . they never do that for me," Sarelli complained as he put his gun back into its holster." He swaggered closer to the threesome. "Hey…why they lookin' at me like that?" Recollection of the stance came slow to the big galoot, but it did register. He went for his gun, but it was too late.

"Kill!" Richard commanded. Like that the dogs were on the giant, much like hyenas on a lion, and no less noisy. Richard hoped Daphne would not hear the ruckus, but if she did, he prayed she would ignore it. Luckily within minutes, which seemed like hours to Richard, the dogs had completed their task. As Sarelli lay unmoving a couple of feet away, Misty and Rex trotted toward their master for their reward. Richard patted them affectionately on their heads as he walked over to the bloodied heap of flesh and flipped him over. His face was mangled. His neck was gone. Richard had already known that would be the case. It was what he had spent months training the dogs to do. But he had to be sure. It took a lot out of him just to drag the big guy's corpse over behind the hedgerow. The aggravation of two dogs yipping at his heels did nothing to promote his mental position.

"Damit! Hush now!" he commanded.

For about a fraction of a second he felt kind sorry for Sarelli. It was too bad he had to die, but there was no other way. He said a quick prayer for the guard's soul, and then went to lock the dogs in their kennel. When he finished, he looked himself over for signs of dishevelment. It was time to go and make sure that Daphne was, and remained, unaware of all that had transpired in the last hour.

****

"Well, I got me a weapon," Bucky joked, as he sauntered out of the kitchen wielding a plastic knife.

"I do not see anything humorous about this situation Mr. Rivers. Must you continue to make jokes?" Helen complained.

"Well, well, Mrs. Klein," Bucky mimed the motion of tipping a hat that wasn't there. "It has been awhile. You haven't changed a bit—still trying to run the show I see, and pretty as ever doing it." He smiled genuinely her way. "I take it that my boy contacted you in his search to find me?"

"No, in fact it was purely coincidental that I came across him," she admitted. Her lips trembled as she went on. "The moment he recognized me, he bombarded me with questions about you. That boy was obsessed with finding you, and his desire inspired me. It is because of him that we have found you and Richard." Tears filled her eyes. "You should be proud Mr. Rivers, he is a fine young man. I haven't the vocabulary to express just what he has come to mean to me."

"Well, it does my ticker good to hear it. Now if we could just get out of here alive, and in one piece, I'd like to judge him for myself."

"Mr. Rivers . . . will Richard be all right?" Helen begged to be reassured.

"I do believe so, little lady."

"Yes Mama, Papa is going to be fine," Rita promised.

"What should we do?" Helen gasped as began to pace back and forth. She walked over to the door and peeked out. "I hope this plan works. I can't see anything from here! Where is he?"

"Get away from there!" Bucky shrieked with much animation. His green eyes looking like they were ready to pop out of his head. "We just need to sit tight and wait for him to get back here," he stressed.

"Yes, but what do we do when he returns?" Helen whined. She looked across the yard again before closing the door.

"Well, *if* he returns, that'll mean Sarelli is out of the picture. Therefore we should be able to hightail it right on outta here!"

Helen resumed her pacing. "If it is going to be *that* easy," she grumbled, "why may I ask, was this plan not tested at an earlier date?"

"Look, this is going to be anything but simple. Luck is somewhat on our side right now considering Biggs and LaCasto are out of town, but taking down Sarelli is not going to be an easy task! If we make it outta here alive we got ourselves a good beginning. Queen of Sheba up there on the hill, well, she's got connections—we'll have to watch our backs every second."

Bucky shook his head pathetically. "You think we enjoyed our stay, do ya? Over the years your old man and I wanted outta here so bad we could taste it, but there were threats to consider. Well, I should say that I didn't have much of anything to consider. Without your old man's help I was a bee without a stinger, unable to defend any real thoughts of escaping. But I'll lay money on it that your old man did. But Daphne, she would never let him forget who'd pay if he ever left—and that would be you, and your pups ma'am."

"He really did want to come home? He didn't want to be with her?" Helen cried joyously.

"Why, hell yes he wanted to go home! He despises Daphne, and has since I met him seems to me. Heck, you didn't have one little thing to worry about pretty lady, back when you thought he was cheating on you. He's the loyalist son of a gun I ever investigated! He was so loyal . . . I damn near couldn't believe it. I figured it impossible that anyone could be *that* loyal. I spied on his ass a lot longer than usual hoping I'd get the goods on him. Only I never did 'cause he wasn't buyin' any."

"I am such a fool," she whimpered.

"Well . . . if we make it outta this mess alive you'll have the rest of your life to make it up to him," Bucky encouraged. "You know what? I can already see a change in him—a bounce in his step, excitement in his eyes. He's only been sucking wind to survive around here, but times they are a changin'!"

"Mr. Rivers, are you excited?" Rita exclaimed. "How can you stand it? I would be jumping out of my skin if I were you. Nathan is going to be thrilled when he sees you."

"Hey there lass, you get a twinkle in your eye every time that boy of mine is mentioned. We got a little Harlequin in the making here?"

Rita blushed profusely. "Sure I like him. He's very sweet. If you want to know anything beyond that, you'll have to ask him."

"Glad to hear you like him. And it pleases me to see you're no blabbermouth!"

"Nathan told me you weren't too keen on people who had a lot to say."

"Well, he's about half right. I don't mind people talkin', just as long as what's coming out of their mouth is worth something.

****

CHAPTER 13

Daphne met Richard at the door. "Where have you been? I just got a call from Max, Joe Welch is dead."

"What?" He paled a little.

"He's dead!" she repeated. "Apparently he hung himself. Max is headed to Michigan to divvy up his estate," she explained as she put her arm in his. "I'm sure he left most of it to me."

"You mean my estate, or what's left of it anyway," Richard snapped.

"Come now love, you have more than you could ever ask for right here," she pointed out. She made a sweeping motion, bringing to his attention her prized belongings surrounding them.

"None of this is mine precious, and you and I both know it," he bit off scornfully. He smiled, but his tone was hostile.

"All of it could have been yours. It's not my fault you went and married that homely woman and ruined everything," Daphne pouted. "You said you loved me, and I told you I loved you too. But you expected me to live on it . . . Sorry love, but I know myself well enough to know that it was never going to happen. I mean really, to live like a farmhand when I'm used to owning the farm! I just couldn't do it." She paused momentarily, took her arm from his and smoothed her skirt. "You think I'm terrible for saying that, I know, but you're no different. You're just as worried about what's yours, and what's not, as I am, or you wouldn't have made that remark about Joe's estate. Aren't you even a little sorry the poor man is dead?"

"No. It's about damn time the sorry son-of-a-bitch did something useful," Richard voiced glacially. He looked hard at Daphne and the hold that he had on his control snapped. He began to walk toward her, his contemplation of what he was going to do to her unmerciful. With each step he felt his anger grow until it nearly blinded him. The cold beauty with all her threats had kept him prisoner for seven long years and he was not going to let her off easy, no, she was going to pay dearly. He grabbed her roughly by the neck, and ushered her into the library.

"What? What do you think you are doing, Richard! Get your hands off me!"

He laughed shrewdly. "Sorry precious."

"Sarelli!" Daphne screamed, while she tried quite pitifully to fight him.

"Scream all you want—your big bad bodyguard is dead."

"No," she cried.

"Yes, and I'm only sorry that I hadn't the guts to do him in a long time ago."

"You won't get away with this, you bastard. If you leave, I'll have you hunted down."

Richard grabbed a hand full of her luxurious blonde mane and pulled her along beside him to the old rolltop desk. With his free hand he opened and rifled through the middle drawer. He found what he had sought, and awkwardly ripped off a piece of duct tape. "Hunt me down, I don't give a damn."

"Richard you know what I can do, you better let me go right now," Daphne threatened. "Glen is going to be here any minute for lunch, and you will be sorry. But . . . if you stop now . . . I'll forget the whole thing."

"Is that so? That's good to know." He fought to put her hands behind her back to bind them. He could have knocked her out, like he had Rita, but he wanted her awake; he needed her to suffer. When he finished with her hands, he taped her mouth shut and dragged her along beside him to the phone.

"Hey there Roberta, Richard here . . . Sheriff in?"

Daphne started to struggle and kick, trying her best to make some noise. Richard pulled hard on her hair to quell her zest.

"You get a hold of him and tell him Daphne is not going to be able to do the lunch thing today—she just got news that a good friend of hers passed away, and she has to leave town," he paused to let Roberta offer her condolences. "Oh, he was one of her suitors back when we were kids. She's heavy hearted this morning, but she'll be all right. I think she just wants to be left alone for awhile." Richard impatiently tapped his fingers on the desk as he listened to the woman on the other end prattle on and on. When she finally finished he rushed to end the call, "Thanks doll, and I'll tell her you offer your sympathies." With that he hung up. After Daphne's little display of theatrics he decided her feet should be tied too, and then proceeded to do it. When he finished, he left her in the library while he went to the basement. He returned after ten minutes with a can of gas, pouring it randomly, dousing every little article the blonde goddess had treasured throughout his years of imprisonment. Daphne began to squirm frantically. Tears poured as she cried desperately, the muffled, mournful sound of it was music to Richard's ears. When he finished drenching the place he hauled his terrified hostage outside and dropped her on her rump in the drive. He went back into the house and within minutes came out toting a painted portrait the bitch had paid so dearly to have done of him.

"Since I have known you, you have had your every fancy granted; first by a drunkard father, and then by men who were too caught up in your beauty and on the surface charm to see you for your evils. I have watched you lie, steal, torture and kill to get your way—usually on a whim. It was out of pure fear that I ended up here with you, and have remained here for so long. Let me just set your high society ass straight. I came here for no other reason than to protect my family. Let me repeat. It was for them that I came here, and it is they whom have prompted me to brave your vengeful wrath to leave. I want you to see with those icy-cold crystal blues of yours the pleasure it will give me to present this painting to the woman it truly belongs to, the one and only woman who ever really possessed my heart."

Richard knew without a doubt there was no one else on the earth that Daphne despised more than Helen, and he was going to stab her black heart with barbs on the subject every chance he got. He walked up to the entrance of the house, lit a match and threw it onto the foyer floor. It ignited with a great whoosh. Flames spread quickly along the gasoline trail, licking at and then quickly consuming the beautiful lace curtains that covered each window in the entryway. Richard watched fascinated as the flames spread, and when he was sure the fire had taken hold, he turned toward his hostage. With the portrait in one hand, he scooped her up with the other and headed toward the guesthouse.

****

"Holy smokes!" Billy yelped, his eyes wide with wonder, "there's a fire!"

"What to hell?" Nathan breathed.

Black smoke stood out starkly against the blue sky over in the direction of Daphne's place. Nathan stepped hard on the accelerator, as his mind raced with all kinds of thoughts of what misfortune might have befallen his lovely Rita.

"That's the old lady's place!" Billy crowed.

"Damned if it ain't, looks like all hell broke loose while we were gone."

Billy's face paled. "Do you think Rita'll be all right?"

"You know your sister Billy, she crosses the "t" in tragedy," he complained. Then in an attempt to soothe the boy's fears he added, "She'll be fine."

With that, Billy seemed to relax a little. Nathan slowed the car as they neared the house because it dawned on him there was no way he could just go cruising up to the house as if he owned the place. He had Billy to consider, and lately the poor kid had been through enough grief to employ the Red Cross for relief. He decided to pull over in the same spot he had left Helen earlier.

"Now where did Mama go?" Billy barked as he scanned the area frantically. "She just got after Rita for running off, and now she's gone and done it too! We gotta go find 'em Nathan. They might be stuck in that fire!"

"Billy I'm not going to take you up there, it's too risky . . ."

"I'll go myself . . . you ain't no boss of me," Billy proclaimed fearlessly.

"Damnit Billy! You'll sit here if that's what I want you to do." He hated to be so gruff with the boy, but it was for his own good.

"Well, at least drive on by," Billy crooned. "Maybe we'll see something."

The kid had a point. The old Falcon started right back up as they inched their way forward toward the drive. From the road, the black smoke seemed to be getting thicker.

"See anything?" Nathan asked as he surveyed the area himself.

"I'll be! There's Papa right there."

"Where? You're crazy, I can't see him."

"In the back, going toward them trees by that cabin, he's carrying something."

"Damn Billy, I don't see a thing?"

"Well, you better get your eyes checked . . ."

"There . . . there's someone," Nathan announced. "You're sayin' you can tell from here that . . . that man back there is your dad?"

"Yep! I'd know my Papa anywhere. Isn't anybody else in this world that walks like he does. Drive on up there!"

"Okay kid . . ." Nathan half laughed, "what do you suppose we'd do if we got up there . . . and the man who could be nobody other than your dad is some goon packing a six shooter? For Pete's sake Billy, if you had a brain you'd be dangerous!"

"Fine! I go it alone," Billy shouted as he fumbled around for the door handle. "Geeze Nathan, you act like you're scared or something. You're a cop, don't you have a gun?" The kid was thoroughly disgusted with his state trooper friend.

Nathan wondered what had brought him to this. At this point he wasn't sure of anything. He knew he could hold his own if confronted, but when it came to keeping the kid safe from harm he had his doubts. He had not expected this segment of the Klein family composition, and it burned him to know that it was, and would be for some time, orchestrated by a little wisp of a conductor known as Rita Lee.

As the car turned slowly into the drive Billy shouted, "Yep, it's Papa all right," and before it came to a complete stop he jumped out. "Papa, Papa . . ." he called out as he raced toward his father.

"What?" Richard screeched as he turned toward the approaching boy. There was no doubt in Richard's mind that the lanky youngster rippin' toward him was his youngest boy Billy. He only wondered ashamedly as he put the portrait and Daphne down, just how he was going to explain to his young son his reasons for having his hostage bound and gagged. "Billy . . ."

"Papa." The boy jumped into his father's arms and hugged him with every ounce of energy his little body could muster. "I knew it was you. I told Nathan . . . ain't nobody else in the world who walks like you." Billy beamed, and then asked unabashedly, "What ya going to do with the old broad?"

"I really don't know son," Richard explained to the boy as he eyed the advancing Nathan warily. Their eyes met, then locked. "I hope you didn't get the police involved."

"Mr. Klein," Nathan addressed the older man as he extended his hand. "I'm Nathaniel Rivers—and no, I didn't involve the locals. I was going to, but the receptionist down at the post mentioned the sheriff was supposed to do lunch at the Rodgers place, so I immediately thought they might be on good terms." The two men shook hands "I don't know how the boy knew it was you, but he did." Nathan shrugged his shoulders. "Where are Rita and Helen?

"They're in there." Richard looked toward the guesthouse then added, "I wouldn't doubt if they all think I'm dead by now. I was supposed do away with her protector . . ." he pointed toward Daphne, "and get my ass back there. But I've got my own agenda . . . I started the blaze. Let's just say it's my way of beginning the healing process."

"Perfectly understandable," the younger man sympathized. He paused for a moment, then nervously asked, "Speaking of agendas . . . you wouldn't happen to know anything about my old man, would ya?

"Who Buck? You look more like brothers than father and son. I can't believe that old prankster has kids—he just doesn't fit the father mold. He sure as hell is going to be happy. Damn!" Richard cursed as he heard the low blare of sirens in the distance.

"Go on!" Nathan ordered. "Take her and Billy back to the guesthouse. I'll occupy the authorities while you hide yourselves. "Go!"

Richard hastily picked up the painted portrait and flung it into the weeds. He scooped up his hostage and headed for the guesthouse with Billy in tow as Nathan headed for the end of the driveway to flag down the fire trucks.

As the first engine on the scene pulled into the drive, two firefighters jumped off the back of the truck and went to work on the hose. The passenger side door of the truck opened and a man called out to Nathan, "Is that your vehicle, son?" Without waiting for an answer the old man snapped, "Can you move 'er?"

After Nathan moved his car he was met by the same firefighter.

"What happened here?" the old man inquired with a surprisingly powerful southern drawl.

"Well . . ." Nathan started. "While I was driving down the highway I saw the smoke. When I got here I saw a bunch of kids running across the yard . . . they were laughing like crazy. They saw me too, and took off into the woods. I thought about following them, but decided it would be wiser to check in the house. I looked around as best I could, and called out several times. I got no answers. I heard the sirens and decided to flag you down. I'm James Brown." Nathan extended his hand and shook the old man's gloved one.

"I'm a volunteer firefighter back home, so I'll do what I can to assist you."

"Welp, I'm Sonny . . . but you can call me Chief, everyone else does. Looks like she's going pretty good. I'd say we'll do good by 'er just to keep 'er from spreadin'"

The old geezer looked to be seventy and frail as hell. He was so bent over Nathan doubted his ability to hold on to a hose, let alone lifting unconscious victims. His doubts were quickly put to rest as he tagged behind the old man with whom he had a hard time keeping up. The feisty fellow obviously kept active in his old age. He gave instructions to the other firemen, then turned fiercely on Nathan. "Do you hear them dogs a yippin'? Why don't you go around back and see if you can find 'em—and let 'em loose . . . I'd hate to see to see 'em end up like a couple of roasters. Watch out though . . . word has it that they're a vicious pair."

"You got it, Chief," Nathan exclaimed as he took off to carry out the order. Due to overwhelming heat of the blaze he had to go way out and around the house. As he rounded the southwest corner he saw a glimpse of red behind the hedge. Upon closer scrutiny he recognized the mass as a body. It had to be the "protector" Richard had talked about. He resented Klein for being so careless and leaving the corpse virtually in plain sight. Now he would have to dispose of it, and the damn thing was huge—a bloody mess. He took off his poncho and wrapped it around the dead sap's head and gored neck. It took every ounce of energy he had to lift the carcass over his shoulder. He tried desperately to keep his balance when the momentum of the action caused him to stagger backward. Through the thick smoke and enormous heat he fought his way to the nearest window and heaved the body against it. Upon the impact glass shattered and the body fell through. Bright orange flames engulfed Nathan and habit caused him to drop to the ground and roll around a couple of times. He knew he had been burned, if only slightly, when the smell of singed hair filled his nostrils. After rolling quite a distance away from the raging fire he lay on his back hacking violently in an attempt to clear his lungs. Completely exhausted he continued to lie on his back against the welcoming cold earth. After a moment he turned to get up and looked toward the guesthouse just in time to see five figures making their way into the trees. He scanned each figure determinedly until his eyes rested on the petite frame of which he sought, only then did he relax a little. He remembered the dogs and impulsively ran toward their frantic barks. When he reached their kennel he noticed they were not in any imminent danger from the fire, so he decided to leave them to someone else's care, figuring it would be best if he made his exit before the sheriff arrived.

"Good lord . . . What happened son?" Chief exclaimed as Nathan neared. The old man looked him over from head to toe, front to back, before speaking again. "I heard the explosion . . . I was hoping you were clear of the danger."

"Luckily I didn't get the full force, it just clipped me. If you don't mind, I'd like to drive on down the hospital to be looked over.

"Don't mind at all . . . Sheriff's on his way, let him give you a lift."

"No! I'm mean . . . ah . . . he'll have other more important things to do." Nathan was fidgety.

Chief laughed, "I don't know where you come from boy, but this is about the most excitement we've had around here all year—this is important. Besides, the sheriff is going to want you to give a description on those kids you saw. You know that pack of kids who supposedly skipped school and decided to torch a 150 year-old house today?" The old man looked hard at the younger man, but there was a glint of understanding in his wise old eyes.

"What kids?" Nathan feigned amnesia. He lowered his head into his hands, and grimaced as though he was in pain.

"Damn good thing the Sheriff didn't make it here first. He'd a hauled your butt to jail on a dime with a story like that." Chief continued quite humored, "a pack of kids runnin' into the woods . . . Ohhhh weee." He laughed. "I've heard it all now. We got tight rein on our youngens' around here boy . . .those things just don't happen . . . Hey, you all right?"

"My head is pounding, but other than that I'm fine. I better get to the hospital . . ."

"You're like a thoroughbred chaffin' at the bit to be off," the old man patted him firmly on the shoulder. "Go on now. Keep a good pace. If you see the sheriff, don't break, just keep on going, nice and steady." Chief walked with Nathan toward his car. "Good luck to you *James Brown* . . . and hey.... Tell Richard ol' Sonny always liked him."

Nathan was floored. "Ah . . . I will," he assured, amazed by the old man's statement. He closed the door and cranked the starter then rolled down his window and called out, "Hey Chief, I never checked the building there in the back hunkered in the middle of those walnut trees. There's no tellin' what I might've found in there."

"We'll have to check 'er out . . . maybe in a week or so. Go on now, boy." Sonny urged before turning away.

Nathan watched the old man walk away and realized that before meeting him he had never wanted to live past the age of sixty for fear that old age only meant infirmity and loneliness. But meeting ol' Sonny dispelled the notion of impending debility, and Rita was the perfect antidote for the loneliness bit. Having finally located his dad he was free to focus on whatever his heart desired, and getting serious with Rita was his desire, even though it was bound to get heavy. He thought about how crazy things had gotten since he laid eyes on the little wretch. In the last week he had been arrested, involved in a murder, nearly burned to toast, barely able to sleep, unable to eat, yet he felt more at peace with life than ever before. A bright white smile flashed across his soot-covered face as he put the car in gear and set out to locate the girl who promoted the peace.

Nathan drove slowly down the dirt road away from the fire toward the spot where he had left Rita and Helen earlier. He saw movement in the brush and sped toward it. Five wild-eyed escapees scrambled out of the woods and approached the car with a purpose. Nathan slipped the Falcon into park and opened the passenger side door as Helen jumped in with Richard right behind her. Rita, Billy and Bucky crammed into the back seat as the Falcon pulled away from the embankment. In disbelief Nathan looked back at his father. Besides the beard, his old man looked pretty much the same. As their eyes met, both smiled simultaneously and reached for the other's hand. There was nothing to say, for everything that mattered was summed up in the look they shared. Nathan turned away to concentrate on his driving. No one said a word as a varied ensemble of heavy breathing filled the compacted car. Nathan had wanted Rita to be in the front seat with him. He wanted to touch her, needed to see for himself that she was all right. For now beholding her countenance in the rearview mirror was going to have to cut it. He grimaced a little as his gaze caught sight of the worried expression on her face, and winced as his focus switched from her to his own reflection. Surprise stole his breath. *Damn,* he thought, *she must think me an ugly cuss.* His face was black with soot, except for the white wrinkle creases at his eyes. Hundreds of tiny white snarls gave proof that his hair was terribly singed. He was a mess, and it bugged him to no end that Rita saw him that way.

"Gosh Nathan what happened to you?" It was just like Billy to send the message home.

"Had a little run in with a raging fire, kid. Don't worry though . . . I have been in hotter situations." He couldn't help but emphasize his point with a bold stare into the rearview mirror, especially for the little fire starter behind him.

She blushed and smiled sultry-like at his totally disheveled reflection. It meant a lot to him that she didn't seem at all offended by his appearance.

Just as they neared the main road they heard sirens approaching. No one dared to move. Nathan remained calm and implored for his passengers to try to act natural, but that was easier said than done. Every one of them held their breath as the speeding police car zoomed on by. The effects of the close encounter left them all drained, and several minutes passed before any of them dared to speak again.

"What are we going to do? Where are we going to go?" Helen whined. "We have to stop somewhere so I can call Ma and let her know what has happened. When they find Daphne, the first thing she'll do is call Joe!"

"No she won't," Richard said softly in an effort to calm Helen.

"Oh yes she will Richard. I know you are not going to believe this . . . You and Joe were always so close . . . But I know for a fact that he is partly to blame for all this . . ."

"Helen, honey, I know that . . . I know all about Joe," he assured.

"Richard he'll find out about what we did . . . and . . . and he'll go straight to Ma's . . . Oh Lord, the children!"

"Joe's dead."

"What?" Helen's face looked bloodless as her jaw dropped open wide.

Rita did not trust what she had just heard. She looked to Billy for confirmation, but he too looked totally confused. They both waited earnestly for what was to be said next.

"They found him dead this morning. He hung himself."

"That's a lie!" Helen gasped, "Joe would never do that, it's got to be some kind of a trick."

"I wouldn't have believed it of him either, but it's true." Richard put his arm supportively around her. "Chalk it up to divine intervention if you must, but believe it, he's dead."

Could Daddy Joe really be dead? Rita wondered. She tried picturing him hanging in the same way she had found Betty a few days ago, and couldn't. It didn't make sense. He just never seemed the type of person who would take his own life. *Then again, neither had Betty.* But Daddy Joe had way too much fun living and making other people's lives a living hell. She saw him as the type of person who would have found a way to drive someone to do the deed for him just so they would have to live the rest of their life paying the consequences of it. And with black eyes shinning he'd be laughing and looking up from his final resting place, relishing his accomplishment.

"It could be a trick," Rita thought aloud. "I wouldn't put it past Daddy Joe to do something like that just to lure us back home . . ."

"Yeah," Billy agreed.

"They could be right," Helen contributed. "Look how easily they made it seem that you were dead Richard—we must be prepared for anything."

"It's no trick." Nathan said in an irritated tone. Up until that moment he had been silent.

Everyone looked at him.

"What makes you so sure?" Helen asked anxiously.

Rita watched Nathan closely. Why was he so sure that Daddy Joe was dead? Did he know something the rest of them didn't? She willed him to look at her into the rearview mirror, but he wouldn't. She wanted to look into his eyes. She would be able to see deceit there if there was any to be found, she told herself. A chill ran up her spine as she remembered the last night that she had seen Daddy Joe alive. Hadn't Nathan rushed them out to the car while he looked around for some rope? No. She would not entertain such ridiculous thoughts. Daddy Joe hung himself. That was that.

"Well I don't know for sure," Nathan said coolly, his face blank as he looked straight ahead at the road. "I just think you are all being a little paranoid about the whole thing. I mean the guy doesn't have that much clout—to pull off that kind of stunt on his own."

"Nathan's right," Richard agreed. "Joe would have needed Daphne's help to pull it off. If it is a trick Daphne was oblivious to it. She thinks he's dead. She never would have sent her lawyer up there if she had believed otherwise."

"Right." Nathan said concluding the subject. "We need to figure out where to go from here. With Joe out of the picture we need to focus on any real threats..."

"You should'a let me take care of the dame like I wanted." Bucky expressed with much regret from the back seat. "It wouldn't have bothered me one bit to do a little time for taking care of her.

After everything she put us through, I could have claimed self-defense for sure. We could have been done with the whole damn mess . . ."

Helen turned and glared at Bucky, "The children!" she scolded.

"Hell little lady, they ain't neither one been too sheltered . . . didn't take me to long to figure that one out. It isn't my fault they're here and I must say that if they were any kids of mine, right about now they'd be breathing heavily into some schoolbooks somewhere up in Michigan. So let's not talk in riddles for their sake, huh? Ain't nothing I hate more'n talking in riddles!"

"Well it doesn't matter now." Richard snapped. "We did what we had to in order to escape with our lives, and we did it without killing needlessly. This will benefit us when we go to the police. As long as we talk to someone who is on the up and up we'll get out of this. Buck, who can we trust?"

"Teeball Graham. Remember 'ol Teeball Nathan? I'll bet he's made captain by now?"

"Yep." Nathan said, "and he's in the running to be the next chief. He'll set us up. Let's just hope we can make it back home in order to solicit his help."

"Hell," Bucky hooted. "We've made it this far . . . ain't nothing going to stop us now."

****

CHAPTER 14

Joe was dead. His body was cremated and his ashes were sent to the Benton Funeral Home in Ann Arbor, where his brother Frank and his wife Olivia received them. They made burial arrangements, and at Joe's memorial service Sheriff Vanderpool made excuses for Helen and Linda. He informed the Welch's of the ongoing investigation and of the temporary relocation of the family. Olivia wondered aloud if the lawyer handling Joe's estate, Max Goodrow, had anything to do with the case. She had thought it odd that he had left town immediately after arriving for unknown reasons.

Teeball Graham was every bit the cop that Bucky and Nathan had claimed that he was. He and his staff worked day and night to end the misery that Daphne Rodgers had caused the Klein and Welch families, among countless others. After cooperating fully with the police, the Klein's, including Richard's parents were relocated. Bucky declined relocation spouting that he'd be damned if he was ever going to be ruled by the actions of the likes of "that woman" ever again.

Nathan went back to work immediately and spent most of his free time helping Teeball and his crew. Teeball was so impressed by his hard work and dedication that he persuaded him to take a detective position in the city of Lansing's Homicide Department, promising better advancement. Nathan made the transfer in hopes that he could devote more of his time to getting Daphne put away. Then he could start his life with Rita.

No one was really surprised to hear news of Daphne Rogers's

death. It was a clean little affair to tidy things up. She was found in her bed, shot in the head by her jealous lover Max Goodrow, who then turned his gun on himself. Teeball knew it was a sham, and wanted to get to the truth, but Nathan didn't care. All he could see was that Rita was out of imminent danger, and he was satisfied with that. He wanted to be the one to tell her it was over. It had been months since he had last laid eyes on her and every second that went by without her just about killed him.

Teeball scribbled an address on a piece of paper, "Go get her Tiger!"

"I planned on it." Nathan said with a smile as he snatched up the paper.

When he arrived at the address Teeball gave him, Helen met him at the door. "Goodness, Nathan, How are you? Come in." She ushered him inside to the kitchen where she hugged him mightily. By this time Richard had appeared.

"Hey there Nathan. Any news?" He said while extending his hand.

"Where's Rita?" was all Nathan could manage, just as the sound of feet pounding on stairs caught his attention. His heart was beating furiously.

"Nathan." Rita cried out as she rushed into his arms.

God it felt so good. Nathan could not believe how nice it felt to have her settled in his arms. "Damn girl . . . I have missed you."

Her arms were all over him. "Oh Nathan . . . I'm so glad you came today. I was going crazy. Do you even know what you have done to me? I don't know how to live without you. I don't know what to do. I thought my life was over . . . I thought that I might never see you again."

"You thought wrong." He gazed down at her lovingly. Her eyes were so bright and crystal clear as she looked back at him. "I want you . . . I mean . . ." He pulled away from her and reached into his pocket, pulled out a little gray box and opened it. It was a diamond ring. The most beautiful ring that Rita had ever seen.

Helen gasped and quickly put her hand to her mouth as Nathan got down on one knee.

Rita laughed nervously as she looked down on him. "What are you doing, you silly man?"

"Rita Lee, will you marry me?"

"Oh Nathan . . . Do you really want to live like this?" She wasn't really asking. "I love you too much . . ."

Nathan stood up, quite exasperated. Rita continued mumbling objections until he silenced her foolishness with a kiss. He knew right then that life with her was never going to be easy. But life without her—well, he just couldn't imagine that.

EPILOGUE

March 9, 1973

The small church was filled to capacity. The scent of Jasmine crept from beautiful yellow flowers. Woody vines meshed through the lattice of the hand carved arbor that Nathan stood fidgeting under. His father stood proudly beside him, smiling from ear to ear as an organ hidden in the balcony of the church blared out the age-old wedding march, silencing the idle talk of the congregation.

Rita was shaking pitifully. She couldn't believe that it was time. She was thankful that Papa was there, solidly beside her. She felt like she might fall over if it wasn't for him. Her gaze roved over the crowd settling occasionally on those whose faces were most familiar. She saw Grandma and Grandpa Klein who sat next aunt Alberta, Mama, Sally, and Linda in the front row. Then Betty and her husband Jimmy and little Allen and Alexandria, and Rick and his wife Barb and their newborn Willy, who sat in the row behind them. Maria and Edward and the rest of Nathan's clan sat in the front few row across from them. But there was one face in the crowd that Rita longed to see and didn't. Where was Billy? He was probably outside flirting with all the girls. *The brat!* Giving up on her quest to spot him she finally set her sights on her husband to be. He was absolutely gorgeous. He looked like a movie star, quite dazzling in his white tux. It was all so much like a dream to her. How could someone so beautiful and as wonderful as him want to marry her? It was just so hard to believe. She would probably live the rest of her life wondering when she was going to wake up. Her eyes filled with admiration as he smiled nervously her way. When she and Papa reached the arbor, the music stopped.

"Who gives this woman away?" The pastor inquired.

"Her Mother and I do." Richard choked out before leaving his daughter and taking his place next to Helen.

Nathan reached out to Rita and drew her beside him as soft notes from the piano filled the little church. A young man with a sweet tenor voice stood in front of the onlookers. Rita eyes shimmered with tears as she recognized Billy. Behind him the sun's rays streamed through bright sections of a stained glass mural of Jesus. Billy's beautiful voice rang out:

> I remember when you talked about boys and love and growing up
> and all the things you'd someday like to do
> I remember singing songs and sleepless nights that seemed so long
> and holdin' on to dreams that never came true
> I remember falling outs and making ups without a doubt
> right and wrongs and I'm sorry's too
> I wont forget the tears and smiles the tribulations and the trials
> and my very best friend it was you
> Today's your day . . . little girl . . . stand up and smile. . . .
> I'd like to say to my best friend as a child
> I wish you all. . . . the happiness there is . . .
> all the joy that life can bring. . . .
> on your wedding day
> and even though we'll grow apart
> you'll always be right here in my heart
> Yes little sister we will grow apart
> but you'll stay right. . . . here. . . . in. . . . my. . . . heart

When the song ended Billy lead the congregation in prayer.

Rita smiled to herself as she bowed her head and said a little prayer of her own.

Thank you God for everything . . . But most of all . . . thank you for Billy, and his prayers.

Printed in the United States
2392